Francesco D'Adamo was born in Istria, 1949, and is currently based in Milan. He's an award-winning Italian writer whose books have been published in a number of languages. Two of his children's novels, *My Brother Johnny* and *Iqbal* have received much critical acclaim, winning him the New York Christopher Award for Adolescents and the Cento Prize in Italy. In 2004, Francesco won the International Reading Association Teachers' Choices Booklist Prize.

Siân Williams has translated work by Dacia Maraini, Lalla Romano, Antonio Tabucchi and Francesco D'Adamo. She founded The Children's Bookshow in 2003, which takes writers and illustrators of children's literature from the UK and in translation on tour to theatres throughout the country each autumn.

Francesco D'Adamo

Oh, Freedom!

Translated by

Siân Williams

DARF PUBLISHERS
LONDON

First published in UK 2016

By DARF PUBLISHERS LTD
277 West End Lane
London
NW6 1QS
United Kingdom

Original Italian edition: © 2014 Giunti Editore S.p.A., Firenze-Milano
www.giunti.it

Text by Francesco D'Adamo

First published in Italian by Giunti Editore in 2014

Cover designed by Luke Pajak

ISBN-13: 978-1-85077-285-9
eBook ISBN-13: 978-1-85077-293-4

Printed and bound in Turkey by Mega Basim

One
Alabama, May 1850

The man with the gourd slung across his back arrived at sunset, followed by a storm. Behind him, threatening black clouds raced rapidly over the plain, unleashing thunder, flashes of lightning and thunderbolts. In a few more minutes they'd reach where he was too.

Little Tommy was sitting on the river bank, legs dangling in the water, trying frantically to retrieve his fishing line. He'd tried in vain to catch something good for supper. But nothing, not even an old shoe.

The green water was teeming with fish. Tommy could see carp and pike and tench and other good things swimming lazily back and forth in the current. Not one had bothered with the worm attached to the waggling hook that shouted out, 'Eat me! Eat me!'

It was a fat, well-fed mouth-watering worm that Tommy had dug up in one of his secret places. Those grubs had never let him down.

This wasn't his lucky day.

And now a storm was on its way. Tommy got scared when there were storms.

But he wasn't chicken, no not him!

He wasn't frightened of water snakes either, nor those snakes hiding in the cotton rows that hissed as soon as you got near.

Once he'd braved a polecat. One afternoon he'd got close to Old Hunk's hayloft. Everyone said the place was cursed and it was better to give it a wide berth, believe you me.

Sure, he hadn't gone into the hayloft, better not run too many risks. But he had gone close, more than all the other children, including the older ones who put on airs and chewed tobacco like the grown-ups who spat at their feet looking thoughtful.

But he was terrified of storms. And Devils too.

The one sauntering up the dusty little track alongside the river just had to be a Devil because he was taking no notice of the downpour about to rage above his head, and was enjoying his walk as if nothing was happening.

He looked like a Devil too. He was so tall, his head seemed to brush the storm clouds; and he was big and fat. The boy was sure his skin was tough as the pecan trees surrounding Captain Archer's house. And the man looked as solid as those pecan trees: there wasn't a wind that could shake him. His worn-out threadbare trousers had seen countless washes in lye, and a big shirt rose up over his belly. He had a bulky bundle tied to a big stick over his shoulder and a gourd slung across his back.

Only Devils wore gourds like that.

But most of all, there was something weirdly disturbing about the man: he was barefoot and limping in the dust.

Something seemed to be wrong with his right foot. Tommy couldn't see clearly because of the haze of the storm brewing and the dust clouds blowing into his eyes.

But that foot was definitely not normal.

It had to be a cloven hoof like the Devil's. Of course it was!

Tommy tried to reel in his fishing line as fast as possible and run away, but the wind tangled it up. He tried to untwist it, but somehow it got wound round his feet. He got up, grabbed the bucket which was for his catch, tried to run, and ended up on his bottom, on hard ground. It was too late.

The Devil had crossed the space separating them in a single leap and towered over him. At the same moment, a terrifying thunderclap shattered earth and sky. It must have been a sign from Heaven.

'The ways of God are infinite,' said the Devil.

Tommy had to admit he had a point.

The Devil glanced into the empty bucket, 'You haven't had much luck . . .'

Tommy had to admit he had a point.

The Devil lifted him up as if he was made of straw, freed him from the fishing line, rolled it up and put it into the bucket, then held out a big paw.

'My name's Peg Leg Joe. What's yours?'

'Tommy . . .' said the boy cautiously holding out his hand, certain that it would be crushed.

'Are you a Devil?' he asked after he'd got his hand back in one piece.

The man squatted on his heels, 'No,' he replied. 'Are you?'

'No way!' exclaimed Tommy.

'Well then,' said Peg Leg Joe, 'we can trust each other.'

Tommy had to admit that was reasonable.

Now the boy could see the man properly, and stared at the wooden leg sticking out of his right trouser leg. So it was not a cloven hoof.

It was strange and worrying, and something he'd never seen before, but not devilish.

'Tell me,' said Peg Leg Joe, 'who's in charge here?'

What a silly question. Captain Archer was in charge, everyone knew that. It was his plantation. Everything you could see all around belonged to Captain Archer: the land, the tobacco, the cotton, the blue sky, the houses, the stables, the animals, the slaves – right up to the edge of the horizon and to the ends of the earth. It was all Captain Archer's.

That was how God wanted it – didn't He?

'Who's in charge over there,' asked Peg Leg Joe pointing at the huddle of little cabins at the bottom of the path bordering the river where the slaves lived – Tommy's family too. The boy thought about it: none of the slaves were in charge of the village.

Every man was in charge of his own house which was how it should be. The boys would grow up to be men and then they would be in charge of their house, while the girls would grow up to be women and carry on obeying, as they should.

Or at least, he'd always thought so, but now he was doubtful. The last time he'd proudly explained his theory, his Mamma had given him a hard slap and his older sister, Aretha, who was annoying, had taken advantage and given him another one.

They all obeyed the Pastor, Jim Kniff, and the rest of the overseers. And the white men and Captain Archer, even though they rarely saw him. They'd also obeyed the white masters, the mistresses and even the young ladies, despite their being women; although no one had seen them except the servants at the big house.

Perhaps Peg Leg Joe wanted to talk to old George Washington, the village elder. Everyone said he was wise and sensible, so they went to him for advice: to settle a quarrel, make peace in a family, or value a pig fairly.

On the other hand, if you were valuing a girl for a husband, Mamma Maria was the one to see, everyone knew that.

'Take me to him,' said Peg Leg Joe grasping Tommy by the hand.

They walked towards the cabins. An angry wind, raising clouds of dust and stubble, beat furiously at their backs. Huge raindrops as big as coins began to hit the ground.

'Let's run!' shouted Peg Leg Joe. 'The storm's here.'

So they took off.

Peg Leg Joe ran very fast, despite his wooden leg.

A lightning flash split the sky, cutting it in two. Then another. And another. Tommy was terrified and tried to run even faster, to get home safely to Mamma and Papa.

'Have you ever found the point of a flash of lightning?'

'The point of a flash of lightning?'

'Yeah! The point of a flash of lightning stays lodged in the earth like an arrowhead.'

'Sure.'

'It's a powerful lucky charm if you ever find one. It wards off evil spells and the Evil Eye. And helps women giving birth. If you put it under straw, it makes calves grow strong with straight legs. And there's nothing better for corns and nagging coughs, believe you me.'

'Does it work with tummy ache too?' Tommy wanted to know.

'Yes, definitely!'

Tommy thought a lightning point sounded very useful.

Peg Leg Joe paused in the downpour. The rain was teeming down into the river now. Wind swept the grass in the fields and bent the tree trunks, soaking them.How long was it since there'd been a storm like this?

Peg Leg Joe looked at the boy with a serious expression, 'Tomorrow,' he promised, 'we'll look for lightning points. You know how many of them have fallen today?'

'Oh?' shouted Tommy.

'It's a promise. But watch out . . . it's very difficult to find them, only a few people have succeeded.'

'I think we'll find them,' said Tommy.

'Yes,' said Peg Leg Joe. 'You're right, I think we will too. And now . . . run!'

When they reached the village, dripping wet, everyone came to the door of their cabins: a stranger with Tommy was a novelty. The women called to one another so as not to miss out.

The men eyed the man's strange gourd and noticed its long handle, which Tommy hadn't seen properly until then, although they were first drawn to the wooden leg, and then the bulky bundle full of his things. A large bottle wrapped in woven maize leaves and stoppered with a cork, peeped out of it.

'Beer!' ran the whisperings. 'Beer!'

If the stranger was generous there would be a big party. As the wind wailed and the rain found its way through the straw roofs, everyone agreed that Tommy, who had brought them the stranger, was really a very good boy, wide awake and full of initiative. They paid his father compliments and imagined that a successful future lay ahead.

Well, they all said, there are no limits to what a boy like him could do!

Two

A visitor's arrival in the village was a rare and exciting event that would be talked about for months to come by the men round the fire in the evenings, and the women while they shucked corn, helped by the children. Each time, the story would be enriched by some extra detail.

Tommy's parents had the honour of putting up Peg Leg Joe in their cabin. Mamma bustled about a great deal, because she had to prepare a special meal for the guest. She set to work, shouting, banging pots and pans, and complaining about Tommy's sisters – including that goody-goody Aretha – because they weren't helping her enough and were lazy good for nothings.

Tommy had been elected hero of the day for bringing the stranger and had permission – to his enormous satisfaction – to lounge about until supper.

At one point he even had the honour to be called into the middle of a circle of men outside who were chatting and spitting tobacco.

The storm had passed. The air was fresh, clean and humid while the first stars were beginning to appear in the sky. The boy was asked to describe once more how he'd met Peg Leg Joe, and how he'd not been in the least frightened, despite that wooden leg, and how, realising that the stranger was lost and clueless, he'd guided him to the village.

Tommy, chest swelling with pride, told the story four times, under the satisfied gaze of his father.

Then Mamma shouted, 'Dinner, you layabouts!'

What a supper! Fried chicken with corn, sweet potatoes and apple fritters, nothing was lacking.

Tommy stuffed himself full to bursting. Even on big feast days they never ate like this.

During supper, Peg Leg Joe said little, but you could feel from what he did say, that he must be a man of great experience. Wise and devout, he must have seen a great many things, more than he wanted to talk about.

Even old George Washington, who had been invited as a particularly dear friend, listened attentively.

No one asked Peg Leg Joe anything about himself though. The adults thought the same thing: a Negro couldn't go around like that, as if it were nothing unusual. He had to belong to someone! Perhaps 'they' were looking for him?

The best thing was not to ask questions and to make sure that none of the white owners saw him or found out he was there.

Peg Leg Joe in return was generous with his bottle of beer which passed from hand to hand, and in the end everyone was full and in a good mood.

After dinner had finished, the stranger got up, stretched, hobbled to the corner where he'd put down his bundles and came back holding the mysterious gourd in his hand.

By that time, the entire village, including those who hadn't been invited to the dinner – and who were very jealous – had gathered in front of Tommy's family's cabin.

Peg Leg Joe took a stool, carried it outside and had Tommy's family sit beside him, with Tommy in the front row. George Washington was placed in the seat of honour.

The gourd with the handle was then raised high over his head so that everyone could see it. Now everyone could see the strings across the handle, four, perhaps five.

'This,' said Peg Leg Joe, 'is a banjo.'

No one knew what that was, but did not want to seem ignorant before the stranger.

That's what Tommy thought, though he didn't feel shy with his friend.

'And what's that?' he asked.

'It's a musical instrument,' explained Peg Leg Joe. 'Listen!'

He plucked the strings running down the handle which ended where the gourd had been cut and re-covered with something that looked like suede. Ringing sounds came out of the banjo, again and again.

'Ohhhhhhhhh!!!' said everyone.

'Listen,' said Peg Leg Joe.

Silence fell. For a moment or two there was just the gentle slap of water against the nearby river bank, the noise of a fish jumping and a breath of wind stirring the tree tops, still wet after the storm.

Then Peg Leg Joe began to sing, accompanying himself on the banjo.

The words went:

Steal away, steal away
Steal away to Jesus
Steal away, steal away home
I ain't got long to stay here.

Even though the man's voice was a bit rough and a bit off key too, it didn't matter. The song was so sweet it touched the heart. And what sounds he could draw from the gourd with strings!

But how did he do it? It was magic!

Everyone listened fascinated – some with their mouths open stupefied – and everyone was moved when the song ended:

My Lord calls me
He calls me by the thunder
The trumpet sound
Within my soul.
I ain't got long to stay here.

Tommy was captivated not only by the beauty of the music and the marvel of those sounds created like magic by such an odd looking instrument, but also by the words.

One phrase struck him especially and it resounded in his head:

I ain't got long to stay here.

Why did it strike such a chord with him? He was fine here, right where he was, in the cabin with Mamma and Papa, and even with those irritating sisters of his. There was the river where he fished every day; and his secret places. There were the animals he tracked in the tall grass, and the bird nests he visited by climbing the trees.

He was fine here, right where he was.

Even if Tommy was still a little boy, he knew there were other things to be discovered. He wasn't silly. There were the cotton fields under the boiling sun, the hard work, sweat; there was the whip, but only if you behaved badly; there were the white masters who you had to lower your eyes in front of and always say, 'Yes, sir, no, sir.'

And there were also the mysterious things which happened sometimes, at night, and which could not be talked about – like when Old Hunk's son, Orbo, disappeared. He was a hothead – everyone said so – and they'd burned down the old man's barn. There was the fear he thought he'd seen in his father's eyes a couple of times, despite his being a brave man.

But Tommy wasn't too sure, perhaps they were just imaginings that he'd invented.

I ain't got long to stay here . . .

Meanwhile, Peg Leg Joe had begun another song which went:

Dark and thorny is the pathway
Where the pilgrim makes his ways
But beyond dis vale of sorrow
Lie the fields of endless days.

After the storm, the night had grown tender and gentle; a big moon was rising in the sky. When the last notes of the song rang out, everyone remained silent, lost in thought. Many of the women were crying and even old George Washington was moved. What they were thinking was anyone's guess.

Tommy's father got to his feet, cleared his throat and said, 'We thank you Peg Leg Joe. It's late now, and tomorrow will be a hard day for everyone.'

Everyone agreed. They said their thank you's and went home.

'You too,' he said to Tommy and his sisters. 'Bed!'

The boy obeyed unwillingly. The evening had been so exciting that he didn't want to go to sleep at all. Then, before going behind the curtain where his straw mattress was, he noticed that not everyone had left. Old George Washington and Sammy, their neighbour – a big fellow as good and fresh as bread – had stayed.

Stretched out on his pallet, Tommy could hear them talking non-stop in low voices. Peg Leg Joe seemed to talk the most.

Every now and again someone interrupted with a question, and he could make out his father's voice and Sammy's. Once it sounded as if Mamma had joined in.

Tommy knew it wasn't good eavesdropping on adult conversations. His father had ordered him to go to bed, to sleep, and he was supposed to be an obedient boy. He knew if they discovered him there'd be trouble. But what was going on was so unusual, and he was very curious.

He slid from his under his covers and peeped across a fold in the curtain dividing his corner from the rest of the cabin. They were sitting around the fireplace bathed in the tender light of the moon and stars filtering in through the window.

Peg Leg Joe talked slowly, his voice a barely audible whisper. Tommy couldn't make out any of his words. After his speech there was a long silence.

Then old George Washington shook his white-haired head in the darkness and spoke clearly, 'You should follow the Guide. He's like Moses and will lead you to the Promised Land.'

'If it's God's will,' said Mamma.

'Amen,' said the others.

The meeting was over. The last guests left. Mamma and Papa retired to bed. Peg Leg Joe curled up in the corner reserved for him.

Tommy continued tossing and turning on his pallet in the silence. Now everyone was asleep; one of his sisters was snoring softly. The boy's thoughts went round in circles. Such strange things he'd seen and heard! Why had the grown-ups met as if in secret? What did old George Washington mean?

But in his mind, he particularly went over the line of one song, the one that went:

I ain't got long to stay here.

When he finally fell asleep, he dreamed about fields of endless days.

Three

Tommy had hardly fallen asleep – or at least that's how it seemed to him – when he was woken up by someone shaking his shoulder. He opened one sleepy eye, closed it again, got another good shake, unwillingly opened both eyes and saw Peg Leg Joe's big face bent over him with a finger to his lips signalling, 'Silence!' The man gestured again, 'Follow me!'

Tommy slid out of bed, came out from behind the curtain, almost bumped into his bucket and followed Peg Leg Joe outside.

'Silence!' Peg Leg Joe signalled again and, running, guided him to the riverbank where they sat down.

Tommy was wide awake now and excited: an adventure! At night! With his new friend!

'You listened to us,' said Peg Leg Joe.

It was not a question.

'Well, not really, but . . .' said Tommy.

As he was a good boy who didn't tell lies – well, hardly ever – he corrected himself, 'Well, perhaps I did, just a little bit.' Then he added, 'I'm sorry.'

Peg Leg Joe put a grass stalk in his mouth and chewed. All around them was the enormous stillness of the night, broken only by the chirping of crickets, running water, the beating of a bird's wings.

Peg Leg Joe looked serious, 'Listen to me Tommy,' he said solemnly, 'I'm leaving tomorrow.'

Tommy's heart fell.

'But I'll come back in a few days,' continued Peg Leg Joe, 'and we'll go on a long journey together.'

'A journey? Where?'

'Your father will explain everything. Do you ever think about freedom?'

'What's that?' asked Tommy.

Peg Leg Joe scratched his head thoughtfully, chewing the grass stalk.

He gestured with a big sweep of his arm, taking in everything around them.

'It's like the birds,' he said. 'They can fly wherever they want to. Or like fish in the water. Who can tell a fish what to do?'

'Nobody,' said Tommy.

'Exactly. Freedom is not having to pick cotton every day, and not having to feel the whip. Most of all, it's something else.'

'What?'

'To be able to look another man in the eye without being afraid, because every one is the same. They are equal.'

'Even if he's white?'

'Even if he's white.'

'But you can't.'

'Yes, you can. Where we're going you can.'

'Where are we going?'

'A place called Canada. All men are equal and there are no slaves.'

'Is it far?'

'Yes, but we'll get there. I'll guide you.'

'I knew it,' squeaked Tommy. 'You're the Guide like Moses who led them to the Promised Land.'

'I'm only going to take you to Canada,' mumbled Peg Leg Joe.

'It's the same!'

'Well, almost. But now listen to me carefully, it's very important. I want you to learn a song. You must learn it by heart. Perfectly. Never forget it. It's the song, not me, which will lead you and your family to safety. Can you keep a secret?'

'Of course I can!' protested Tommy.

This business was getting more interesting by the minute, a secret now as well!

'What I'm going to teach you isn't a simple song, it's really a secret map which will lead us to the Promised Land. When we sing it, we'll always know the right direction to go in. But no one except us will understand.'

'Gosh,' said Tommy.

'Yes. And do you know how to follow the road to the Promised Land without ever making a mistake, or getting lost? Look!'

Peg Leg Joe pointed a finger up at the immense vault of the starry heavens. 'Look. Look. Do you see those four stars which make the shape of a ladle?'

'Where?' asked Tommy.

'There. Can you see them?'

'Yes,' said Tommy, 'they look like the ladle attached to the rope at the well, where we go to drink.'

'And there's the handle, see it? That long handle ends in one star that's brighter than the rest.'

'Got it!' shouted Tommy. 'That's it. It really looks like the water pump handle.'

What a lot of things there are in the sky, all those strange shapes.

'You must always follow that star,' said Peg Leg Joe. 'Listen.' He began singing under his breath so no one would hear:

When the sun comes back
And the first quail calls
Follow the Drinking Gourd
For the Old Man is waiting for
To carry you to freedom.

'Who's the Old Man?' asked Tommy.
'The Old Man is me . . .' muttered Peg Leg Joe.
'But you're not old!'
'I am too! Pay attention! What must you always do?'
'Follow the Drinking Gourd!'
'Together.'

Follow the Drinking Gourd . . .

'And now,' said Peg Leg Joe, 'you must learn the whole verse. Repeat after me.'

It didn't take much, Tommy was quick and in a few minutes had learned it perfectly.

'When I come back,' explained Peg Leg Joe, 'I'll teach you the other verses. They're important. You must use them every time you find yourself in difficulty on the journey. It's our secret. Here's my hand on it.'

Tommy was very proud.

'And now . . . bed!'

But Tommy didn't move.

'What is it?' asked Peg Leg Joe.

'But you promised me a lightning point to protect me from the Evil Eye and from the runs,' protested Tommy.

'Oh yes! I promised you that we'd look for one together, but you know it's not possible right now. They're waiting for me somewhere else and I can't let them down. Though I know where you could find one. You know the little oak tree wood on the other side of the river, right after the bridge? I crossed it when I was coming here yesterday. There's a forked oak tree in the clearing. Dig where the biggest root is, right under the woodpecker's nest. You'll find the lightning point there.'

'Really?'

'Really. And now . . .'

'Bed!'

Four

P eg Leg Joe had hardly been gone – he had started walking before sunrise – and Tommy was already missing him.

It was a bit silly when he hardly knew him, but he thought of him as his best friend. To confide the secret of the song in him meant that Peg Leg Joe trusted him, didn't he? Even if Tommy was only just ten, he was clearly big enough to help during the long journey awaiting them.

Yes, he was his friend!

As he made his way towards the little oak tree wood in search of the lightning point, Tommy's head was full of thoughts.

Like every other morning, at first light of dawn, everyone was sleepy-eyed around the breakfast table. Him, Mamma, Papa, goody-goody Aretha and Daisy Mae, his other sister.

Like every other morning, they'd said grace, eaten a bowl of porridge, and then Mamma, Papa and Aretha had gone out to begin their work in the cotton fields. Daisy Mae was left in charge of the kitchen.

Sometimes Tommy had to go with them. So he knew from experience how hard the work was and how relentless the sun was, especially now summer was coming.

In the evening they would come back tired and sweaty with backs and arms aching; their legs swollen by insect bites.

Jim Kniff the overseer, who was as hard as a piece of pecan wood, had probably threatened them from horseback as he went back and forth across the fields. Perhaps he had cracked his whip because someone, in his opinion, was slacking.

It had always been so, every blessed day that Tommy could remember in his short life. Yet that morning, the usual actions had a strange effect on him. He had watched as his family took down their straw hats to protect them from the burning-hot sun and put the sacks, in which they would collect the cotton balls, over their shoulders. He had looked at all the other slaves in the cabins nearby making the same preparations, then filing in a long line along the path to the plantation.

He had thought about freedom and the things Peg Leg Joe had said to him the night before. And about that place where there were no slaves – what had he called it? Where you could look in a white man's face as if you were his equal.

Just imagine! No one ever looked at Jim Kniff's face. Better not.

Tommy went along the river.

Could someone tell a fish what to do?

Could Jim Kniff threaten a fish with his whip?

He'd really like to see that!

At the thought, Tommy burst out laughing.

As soon as he saw the wooden bridge and the oak wood on the other side, he focused on finding the lightning point. With that kind of lucky charm you'd never be afraid of anything.

With the exception of the Baron, that is, who roamed the cemeteries at night. Lucky charm or no lucky charm, it was better to avoid him.

And it was better to avoid the crossroads at sunset because Mamma Brigitte was very greedy for children. Tommy wasn't very sure that the lightning point would keep her away.

He would ask Peg Leg Joe when he returned. And also . . .

The boy ran across the bridge, feeling the sodden wooden planks vibrate under his feet, and he slipped into the wood.

It would have been more fun to go hunting for the lightning point with his friend, but he understood that he had made promises to be elsewhere.

But how could he know for sure that the lucky charm was under the forked tree?

Tommy knew the wood, so he found his way easily. In a few minutes he came to the clearing. The forked tree had always fascinated him; it was enormous, twisted, imposing. Had it been there forever? It seemed as old as the world. A huge force must have struck it, splitting it in two from top to bottom.

Tommy picked out the biggest of the gigantic roots which anchored it to the ground, found the woodpecker's nest, moved aside wet leaves covering the earth and began to dig.

Nothing. No lightning point.

Could Peg Leg Joe be wrong?

Tommy scratched his head, wiped his nose on his shirt, got hold of a dry branch and went on digging, using it as a shovel.

There it was, the lightning point!

It looked exactly like an arrowhead, and it was precisely where Peg Leg Joe had buried it that morning, before sunrise, though Tommy didn't know that. He picked it up full of awe, cleaned off the damp earth, and sat down on the oak tree root, clutching it tightly. He felt strong and secure with the lightning's power in his hand.

He thought of the long journey that lay ahead, and of where they would end up – what was the place called? – where everyone was free.

Follow the Drinking Gourd . . .

The Oaks and Captain Archer's estate where Tommy and his family lived and worked were all he knew of the world. Nothing else.

He hadn't even seen all of the estate: it was so big, no one knew where it ended, and what was beyond its borders. They said you could walk for days and days but all you'd see was Captain Archer's land.

They said he owned hundreds of slaves and that there were many other villages of hovels like the one where Tommy and his family lived.

Perhaps beyond The Oaks there was nothing else, except Paradise where everyone went when they died – if they'd behaved themselves, of course.

Another place the boy had heard about was called Africa, but no one knew much about it, not even Papa. The father of his father had spoken of it. Tommy had almost no memory of his grandfather, because he died when he was little.

He had said they all came from Africa and the fathers of their fathers had lived there. He said they should all go back there.

But Peg Leg Joe had mentioned a place called Canada, he now remembered, not Africa. Perhaps they were the same thing.

Tommy walked back home clutching his lightning point tightly. He'd promised Mamma to feed the chickens and shuck the corn for supper.

Too many thoughts were running around in his head.

The journey, the song, freedom . . .

Follow the Drinking Gourd . . .

Despite the lucky charm, he was afraid.

A picture in his head kept on coming back, and couldn't be chased away: Jim Kniff following them on horseback, armed with a whip and a gun, because he was not going to be at all happy about their running away.

Oh, no.

Five

That same evening after supper, Papa said, 'Listen.' He looked very tired and serious. 'Children, listen to me.'

Three pairs of eyes fixed on him attentively. Papa was a simple man, of few words; he wasn't in the habit of making speeches. That evening, clearly, he had something important to say.

'When the stranger, Peg Leg Joe, comes back, we'll leave with him on a long journey. Sammy and his young wife Sarah will come with us too. No one else must know. Peg Leg Joe will be our guide. He knows a secret road which others have travelled before us and he'll lead us to the country Canada where we'll be free.'

Papa paused, wanting to say something more, but it wasn't easy to find the words. Mamma reached across the wooden table and squeezed his hand.

'Yes,' said Papa. 'Let's all hold hands.'

Tommy and his sisters obeyed.

'Let God guide us and bless us.' Papa went on, 'I don't want my children to grow up as slaves. Now let's sing a song together.'

They got up still holding hands.

Mamma struck up one of the hymns they sang in church on Sundays, and everyone joined in with her:

Oh Canaan, sweet Canaan
I am bound
for the land of Canaan.

After the hymn they felt comforted. But the fear of leaving their home in a few days – the village, friends and all the things they knew and loved – to go on a long uncertain journey full of dangers, remained.

'Can I bring my Sunday dress?' Aretha wanted to know.

'I don't want to come,' whined Daisy Mae.

Even Tommy couldn't manage to chase away the scary image of Jim Kniff on horseback.

He remembered that the Promised Land for which they were headed was called Canada, not Canaan, but perhaps it was the same thing.

'When will Peg Leg Joe come?' he asked.

'We don't know,' replied Papa, 'we're waiting.'

The whole week the air was electrified with anxiety and tension. Even Mamma was agitated though she tried to hide it by busying herself with getting some delicacy ready for supper from the few things left in the store cupboard.

Tuesday . . . Wednesday . . . Nothing happened.

On Thursday, Tommy tried to cast an evil spell on his sister Aretha, using the powers of the lightning point, but he must have done it wrong because it didn't work. She realised he was up to something, and slapped him. When he went to complain to Mamma, he got another one. Tommy decided not to trust women because they always stick together.

On Friday evening Papa looked straight at him and gave a small nod: Peg Leg Joe was coming.

Tommy spent all of Saturday morning sitting on the river bank, not even trying to fish. He just looked at the water flowing, the fish jumping, the oak wood and the green line of tilled fields in the distance. Up to that moment, that had been his world. Briefly, his heart ached at the idea of abandoning it.

But then he thought of all the marvellous adventures waiting for him; all the new places he would visit; and all the strange and mysterious things he would discover. He couldn't wait to get on the road.

Then he thought about how wonderful and strange it would feel to be free.

Follow the Drinking Gourd . . .

That evening they had a cold, light meal. Mamma gathered their things into three bundles since they owned hardly anything. She put in some sweet potato she'd already boiled, maize, dried meat, a big loaf of bread she had sliced the night before. Papa filled two gourds with water.

Tommy put his fishing line and the lightning point in his pocket. That was all he'd need on the journey.

There was a knock at the door. Sammy and Sarah swiftly came in. The young wife was still like a little girl. Her big dark eyes were wide with nervousness and fear. She went and stood next to Mamma as if seeking protection. The pair also had two bundles.

When would Peg Leg Joe arrive? What if someone had been spying for the master? Had someone noticed anything out of the ordinary? If a white man had passed by the cabins for some reason . . . But no! White men never passed by the slaves' village and no one – most definitely! – would ever betray them. The slaves were brothers to one another. Yes . . . but if . . .

Peg Leg Joe appeared at nightfall.

He seemed bigger than before, as he filled up half the cabin with his big body.

It wasn't the right time for a celebration.

'Quick!' he said. 'Tonight we must run as fast as prairie dogs. At first light we need to be as far away as possible from here, because tomorrow morning Captain Archer and his men will realise you've disappeared and will come looking ...'

'Perhaps they'll have pity on us?' asked Sarah.

Peg Leg Joe shook his head, 'No way, lady. Don't kid yourself. They won't show any mercy, they'll be furious. They'll chase us like they hunt rabbits. That's how it is, I know. But if you prefer to stay ...'

'We're coming,' said Sammy looking resolute, and he hugged his wife.

'Tomorrow it's the Lord's Day. Because of that they won't notice your absence until it's the service. That gives us a few hours advantage,' concluded Peg Leg Joe. 'We must use it. There's no time left. Stay in a group and take care no one gets left behind. May God protect us.'

'Amen!' replied everyone.

Moments later they were outside, on the dusty little path that cut through the village of cabins. They heard no voices, nothing; neither the usual clatter of pans in the kitchens, nor children's voices. It was as though everyone had held their breath. Candlelight flickered faintly here and there through wooden shutters.

Even the dogs didn't bark as they went by.

Only Skip, the mongrel belonging to Saul, the lame man, accompanied them for a short stretch of the road, rubbing against Tommy's legs. But he finally sat down in the dust and watched them go, as they slipped into the night like ghosts.

They ran under cover of the bank, crossed the wobbly bridge one at a time, vanished into the oak wood, disappearing into the enormous shadows of the trees, then came out again into the open.

None of them had ever gone so far on Captain Archer's estate.

Tommy raised his eyes to the sky, turned his head this way and that, and for a moment was overcome by confusion and giddiness. The sky was too big and black. He couldn't conceive the number of stars, there were so many.

Then he saw it, there it was, how had he not noticed it before?

The Drinking Gourd!

It was where it should be with its handle, in the middle of the sky's endless vault. At the end of the handle was the most brilliant star of all. They were going in exactly the direction it indicated.

Follow the Drinking Gourd . . .

Six

How many hours had they been walking in the darkness of the night?

The march was slow and difficult because they had to avoid roads. The sight of a village nearby, the outline of a farmhouse in the distance, or of a fence marking the boundary of an estate was enough to make them abandon even the smallest of paths to take long tortuous diversions through fields, stubble and scrub; ankles sinking in loose clods of earth, stumbling in the dark, getting scratched.

Peg Leg Joe marched at the head of the column and sniffed out the way like a bloodhound. Every so often he would turn, look around, smell the air, and say, 'This way.'

Every now and again he whispered, 'Watch out!'

Everyone knew they had to curl up on the ground to make themselves as small as possible and melt into the night shadows.

Or he would say, 'Quick, quick!' and they would run for the nearest shelter.

Tommy walked alongside him, next came Papa, then the group of women and Sammy brought up the rear.

The night was clear and sweet, the air fresh and the countryside about them gave an impressions of peace and quiet with its neatly tended fields, irrigation channels, rows of trees, apple orchards and hay stacks.

It was a reassuring landscape which they were used to.

And yet, despite appearances, everything and anything represented danger. Every unexpected sound could be an alarm signal.

The melancholy songs of the night birds, the predators fleeing as they went by, the barking of dogs in the farmhouses followed them for miles.

Once, they heard a man's rough sleepy voice quite clearly, as if he were alongside them, 'Blasted animal! What's got into you? Be quiet and let me sleep!'

'Quick! Quick!'

Tommy tried to look around while they were walking, because it was the first time he'd been able to see a bit of the world, and he didn't want to miss out. But he had to run to keep up with Peg Leg Joe's long relentless strides. And they'd entrusted him with the biggest bundle which became heavy. He was sure it would make his arms break in a little while. That bit of the world he did manage to glimpse didn't seem much different from the one he knew already, and he was surprised. It wasn't as if he was a scaredy cat – not him! – but he was beginning to regret his cabin and the little corner behind the curtain. He would have preferred to be at home still, fast asleep and tomorrow morning go to the river with his fishing line to see if some fine fish or other could be caught.

He didn't want any more adventures, or to see strange new things, no thank you, things were just fine . . .

'Stop!' whispered Peg Leg Joe. 'Everyone on the ground!'

They left the path, headed into the field below, and lay down in the middle of the alfafa which was tall and lush at that time of year.

'Down! Stay down!'

'What's happening?' whispered Tommy in Peg Leg Joe's ear.

'Listen!'

He heard nothing. A cloud covered the moon and the country path was a well of darkness.

'Shhh!' muttered Peg Leg Joe.

Then they heard the bell coming at them out of the darkness. It grew louder and clearer. There was a creaking sound and a horse snorted.

A lopsided cart emerged from the shadows, drawn by a nag which moved forwards very slowly, the bridle unloosened and his muzzle lowered.

He was in no hurry. The bell attached to his harness jingled at every step.

The man seated on the box swayed at every jolt. He seemed to be asleep; head sunk on his chest and the reins slipping from his hands.

The smell of whisky was so strong it reached them in the middle of the alfalfa.

The horse stopped for a moment, looked around, snorted a kind of 'hello', and went patiently on his way. Doubtless, he knew his way home.

'What a scare,' said Tommy. 'It was only an old horse!'

'Let's have a short stop,' proposed Papa. 'Mamma's tired and we all need a bit of a rest.'

'Yes, please!' chorused the girls.

Peg Leg Joe looked nervously at the sky, then peered at the horizon.

'Only a few minutes,' he said. 'We must be at the first Station while it's still dark. It'll be a disaster if someone sees us, they'd realise immediately we're runaway slaves and we'd be done for.'

The grass was soft and pleasant and everyone let themselves relax. A bundle was opened and the provisions prepared by Mamma and Sarah were devoured.

Tommy realised he had quite an appetite. 'How do you always know how to find the right road?' he asked with his mouth full.

Peg Leg Joe finished his sweet potato in two gulps. 'The road we're following is called the *Underground Railroad* . . . it's called that because it's a secret way. It's no good trying to find it on a map 'cause it's not marked. Useless asking around, no one knows about it. The white masters must never find out about it. Only a few Guides possess the secret. Hundreds of brothers before us have already travelled it and reached freedom.'

'Is it the road to Canaan?' asked Sammy.

'Yes sir! It's the road to Canaan, and the Promised Land and Canada where we can finally say, "this will be my country 'cause here all men are equal before God."'

'So you're a Guide?'

'You bet I am! This is the third time I've travelled the old Underground Railroad. With God's help, the white pursuers haven't caught me yet. I was once a slave, and survived every hardship. My master was a cruel, wicked man. I made the same journey you're now making, with a Guide and eleven others. It was a terrible time because our pursuers intercepted us when we were already in Ohio. We thought, "Thank God the end's in sight," but were mistaken. They had dogs and guns, and found us.

We were hunted like animals. They followed us non-stop for three days. One morning they trapped us in a valley. Only four of us, besides the Guide, made it to Canada. My brother had left with us. He didn't get there. Now I'm a free man. I was taught all the secrets of the Underground Railroad, and then I became a Guide. Give me another potato.'

There was a silence. Peg Leg Joe chewed noisily.

'Will they follow us with dogs and guns?' asked Papa.

'You can bet on it. It's why we must put as much distance as possible between them and us. The first Station is still a long way off. We'll find food there, water, and somewhere to sleep. We must rest. We'll only travel at night.'

'What's a Station?' asked Tommy.

'Any safe place can be a Station. A farmhouse, a cowshed, a barn. Sometimes it might even be a haystack. There are also friends ready to help us there. Sometimes they'll put us up, other times they'll simply pretend not to see us. Or at the very least they'll leave a loaf of bread, some cheese, some dry clothes if we've run into a storm . . . from here to Canada. Almost always. Someone will let them know we're coming.'

'How will they let them know?' asked Tommy.

'You ask too many questions,' reproved Papa.

'Nooo. Tommy's an intelligent, curious boy . . . Look,' Peg Leg Joe bent over him as you do when you want to tell someone a secret. 'There are many ways of getting news out there without drawing attention. For example . . .' and he pointed with his big index finger to the banjo he had not taken from around his neck the whole journey.

'With that?'

'Sure! Who notices a Negro in the shade of an oak tree, strumming a stupid Negro song? Who takes any notice of the innocent words he is singing?'

'Yay!'

Follow the Drinking Gourd . . .

'We call it the grapevine telegraph. It sounds like idle talk, nonsense, nothing important. Like when everybody's sitting together on the threshing floor in the evening after a day's work, enjoying the fresh air while they're waiting for some corn on the cob for supper. Or when you go to the shop with the cart to get flour and barrels of molasses, lengths of muslin, and anything else they use at the farmhouse. You waste a bit of time, take it easy, don't you? There you are, leaning on the counter, looking at all the stuff hanging everywhere, enough to make your head spin, inhaling the smells of cinnamon, tobacco, gunpowder. You can meet your neighbours and swap news, who's dead . . . who's had a baby. Chat like that. But the person who needs to understand, understands. It works very well, I can tell you, and the whites don't understand a thing.'

'Brilliant!' shouted Tommy.

'Quiet!' said everyone.

Peg Leg Joe got up, brushing off the bottoms of his trousers. It was the sign that they had to get going. They wrapped up their bundles.

'From now on, save all the breath you have, you'll need it. We must get beyond the hills before dawn.' He turned to Mamma, 'How are you, ma'am?'

'Fine,' she answered, though she was a bit pale.

Papa went to her side.

'Let's go!' ordered the Guide.

Seven

The first Station they reached was in a clearing on the edge of a big holm oak wood. It was a simple hunters hut, built of rough tree trunks with a roof made out of branches. The inside was completely bare, not even a chimney but just a simple fireplace made of stones in the centre of the beaten earth floor of the one room.

Someone had left a goatskin of fresh water, some biscuits, and a piece of salted meat stiff as leather which Papa cut into strips with his jack knife to make it edible. The grapevine telegraph had done its job.

It wasn't safe to light a fire, so they ate a cheerless, cold meal. No one wanted to talk as they were tired, starving, and stunned by recent events.

The last stretch of road they'd had to cross, up and down wild hills swept by an irritating wind, had been particularly difficult and demanding. The terrain was uneven and full of potholes that were dangerous in the dark. When dawn arrived, to risk journeying on with the first rays of sun was worse, since the risk of being seen was even greater. To get to the Station, the last stretch had been out in the wide open.

'Faster! Faster!' Peg Leg Joe kept spurring them on.

The floor onto which they collapsed to sleep after eating was hard and a bit dirty, but to everyone it seemed like a feather bed.

Peg Leg Joe took the first turn on guard, Papa the second, and Sammy the third.

'I want to take a turn too,' protested Tommy.

'OK, you do the last one,' said Papa.

Tommy, now satisfied, wedged himself between Mamma's body and his sisters'. Sleeping together was nice because they were soft and warm, and he fell asleep in a flash. Luckily, no one woke him up for his turn on guard.

The overseer Jim Kniff was furious.

His ruddy face, sunburned from riding horseback, was even redder than usual, and his hard, bristly jaw was like stone.

Better steer clear of Jim Kniff when he was raging, everyone knew that.

That morning he had turned up in church for the service, as he did every Sunday, holding his big white cowboy hat in his enormous hand, his boots shining and a gold chain across his waistcoat. Once a month, before the service, Jim Kniff had a bath and perfumed himself.

As he entered, it only took one look around the enormous nave, immersed in shadow, for him to realise that something wasn't right. He had a sixth sense for these things.

He had done a quick head count of the families standing at the back of the church in their clean Sunday shirts, behind the pews reserved for Captain Archer's family, the white workers employed on the estate, and friends who visited every Sunday.

Jim Kniff also had a reserved place, right behind the family's pew. Although he wasn't a refined man, and spent his life on horseback and stank of the stables, he did hold a very important position at The Oaks. Captain Archer would occasionally invite him for a meal, generally without the ladies. He had five men under his command, and they were only just enough. Jim Kniff had to be everywhere, to know, see and hear everything.

He had to take care of the Negroes; ensure they didn't slack, make them behave and intervene whenever someone got uppity, or a young hothead got the wrong idea. As did old Hunk's son, Orbo.

Jim remembered very clearly the night he had gone to catch him by torchlight with three of his boys. After that he never gave them any more problems.

He counted those Negro heads, all alike and full of lice, in the cool half light of the church: two were missing and their brats with them.

They'd cleared off. He couldn't believe his eyes. They must have gone mad if they thought they could get away with it. Something like this had never happened on the estates where he had been overseer before Captain Archer employed him.

Never.

Every now and again he'd heard stories going around about some Negro who had run away for no apparent reason.

Who knows what went on in those lice-ridden heads. A Negro who ran away hadn't a hope of making it. He wouldn't even manage to survive; neither him, nor his wife, nor his snotty kids. Negroes were stupid and lazy and didn't know how to do anything unless someone gave them orders. You always had to explain things three times before they understood.

Once, a Negro had escaped from an estate twenty miles to the south of The Oaks and had been caught after a week. He had been hiding in a pigsty and smelled worse than usual.

Before giving him what he deserved, someone had asked him why he had done it. As if a Negro could think and understand the reasons for his actions! But somebody did ask him that.

The captive was on his knees, trembling and dribbling because he knew what was coming to him. Then he whimpered he'd done it because he wanted to be . . . free!

Everyone laughed out loud: a free Negro – imagine!

But Jim Kniff hadn't laughed. He went about with his ears pricked up and heard many stories. He knew that there were white men – the renegades! – who said Negroes were men like everyone else, and that slavery should be abolished and they should be free men.

Who could believe such things?

Someone even said that sooner or later there would be a war because of it, but Jim didn't believe that. A war over slaves? Impossible.

There was a handful of Yankee renegades in the North, city gentleman used to going about in horse-drawn carriages who'd feel ill if they set foot in a stable and a bull were to drop a pancake. Pooooh!

But some things shouldn't be mentioned; some ideas were dangerous. Because it might happen that some Negro would actually believe them and then there'd be trouble.

Jim Kniff also knew that Negroes escaped from farms where the masters didn't keep a sharp eye on things, but were lenient and soft.

On The Oaks estate though, at least up 'til now when he was there, such things wouldn't happen. He would recapture them and give them a lesson to remember. He sent someone to inform Captain Archer, got four men together, gave orders to saddle the horses, hooked his spurs to his best boots, rolled the whip round the pommel of the saddle, and carefully loaded his shotgun.

He took off his white cowboy hat and put on his dirty, greasy hat which he had worn every day come rain or shine, during the long campaigns against the Indians, when he rode alongside Captain Archer in his role of scout.

Great times: a buffalo tongue was worth a dollar and an Indian's scalp fifty cents.

They'd finally killed off all of them.

The dirty, greasy hat was a symbol, and had a clear significance for anyone who knew Jim Kniff.

'Let's go get them! Unleash the dogs!' he ordered.

When Tommy opened his eyes it took a moment to grasp where he was.It was neither dark nor light, and in that unfamiliar place there were no windows. He couldn't work out if it were dawn or evening.

The others were already up and murmured quietly in a corner. He got to his feet unwillingly and ate something leftover from the morning.

'In a couple of hours,' Peg Leg Joe announced, 'it will be dark enough and we can get on our way again. Listen: we must reach the Tombigbee river which crosses the forest. It won't be easy walking in the dark. When we get there, we won't find a Station to welcome us 'cause there are none. We'll camp out. Get ready.'

As the women packed up the bags, Peg Leg Joe took Papa and Sammy aside and said to them in a low voice, but not so low that Tommy couldn't hear, 'Be on guard. They'll be on our tracks by now. Even around here. They'll raise the alarm in all the farms in the area. Be on the lookout, they'll say, for runaway slaves, they're dangerous. Many farm owners will want to help them and will take part in the hunt. Almost everyone around here has slaves. If word gets out that us Negroes can run away and not get caught . . .'

'We'll be on our guard,' said Papa.

'If the worst happens, grab your family and scatter. They can't follow everybody,' added Peg Leg Joe.

'And you?'

'I can take care of myself.'

Peg Leg Joe then sat on the floor in a corner of the hut, picked up his banjo and called Tommy to come and sit by him.

'Listen!' he said, looking deep into the boy's eyes, 'I'm going to give you a very important task, but I know that I can trust you. Is that right?'

'You bet!'

Tommy liked it when he was given important tasks.

'Listen. Over the next few days, I can't always be with you . . .'

'But you promised . . .'

'I'm going on ahead to find Stations and organise your shelters. Someone has to know the route and guide the group in the right direction. You'll be the one to do it.'

'But I don't . . .'

'Yes, you do. The songs, remember? I've told you they're a map, they hold all the information you need to get to freedom. You just have to know the secret code. Now I'm going to teach you the other verses. That way you'll always be able to join up with me again.'

Tommy was frightened by the responsibility, but he loved secrets.

Peg Leg Joe plucked the banjo strings very softly, so that no one outside could hear. He sang:

The river bank
Makes a good road
The dead trees
Show you the way
Left foot
Peg foot, travelling on
Follow the Drinking Gourd . . .

'Did you understand?' asked Peg Leg Joe.

'I'm not quite sure,' stammered Tommy.

'It's easy! When we've reached the Tombigbee river you must always follow it upstream. Always, until you get to its source. Each time you come to a fork in the river, and don't know which way to go, to find the right direction, look for the nearest dead tree. I've carved my footprints on the bark. That's the way you have to go, without hesitating. Look!'

Peg Leg Joe pointed to the beaten earth floor on which they were sitting. Clearly marked in the dust were the prints of Peg Leg Joe's left shoe, and alongside it, the circular mark left by his wooden leg.

'That's the sign, got it? When you see those two marks, it will mean that I've gone that way.'

'It's easy!' said Tommy.

'I told you, didn't I? Now listen to the third verse . . .'

The river ends
Between two hills
Follow the Drinking Gourd . . .
There's another river
On the other side
Follow the Drinking Gourd . . .

'I've got it!' Tommy exclaimed happily. 'After we've followed the first river we follow another one.'

'Exactly right, well done! When you've reached the source of the Tombigbee, you'll see a mountain, Woodall, which has a peak with two points which is how you'll recognise it. Always follow the Drinking Gourd and on the other side you'll find a new river, a bigger one, which is called the Tennessee . . .'

'I won't remember all those names,' Tommy protested.

'Nooo! The names aren't important, you've got the Drinking Gourd and my footprints, they'll be enough. But I haven't finished.'

'Oh?'

'No, the journey's not over yet. There's a long way to go. And at the end there's freedom. There's one more verse to the song.'

'Tell me!'

'When it's time. When freedom's really close. Now . . . on the road!'

Eight

'How much further?'

'We must get to the river,' replied Peg Leg Joe. 'We can rest there.'

'Thank God!'

At that moment they heard neighing nearby.

'Don't move!'

They stood stock still.

Nothing but the sound of the wind in the leaves of the trees. A horse neighed and another snorted. They seemed to be at the edge of the wood. Perhaps they weren't the search party. Perhaps travellers were just passing by. Perhaps . . .

But no one travelled at night in these parts if they could avoid it.

Then the sound of barking dogs exploded into the air, a great pack of them, and a rough voice shouted, 'They've caught the scent, they're near here!'

'Run,' hissed Peg Leg Joe. 'Run like you've never run in your life. We've got to reach to the river before them whatever happens.'

Papa grabbed Mamma, almost lifting her off the ground with one arm. Tommy gripped his sisters' hands and ran, ran, ran like never before.

They skidded across slimy ground sloping down to the river; slithered and stumbled over stones and tree roots; fell, got up again; slipped through bushes which scratched their faces and hands. The barking of the dogs rang in their ears and a knot of fear gnawed at their stomachs.

Peg Leg Joe was ahead of everyone and showed the way. Despite his wooden leg, he ran with huge strides and the agility of a prairie coyote.

'Faster! Faster!'

Tommy thought his head would burst. Fear made him blind and deaf. He could barely look where he was going, nor think, nor breathe.

He knew the dogs following them, he'd seen them in the pens where Captain Archer kept them and they weren't like the mongrels, all skin and bone, which used to come into houses in search of a morsel and who were always ready to play. No. These were fearsome hunters, trained to find their prey – be it a stag, or a slave – and show no mercy.

Tommy had heard stories, which children shouldn't hear, about what happened to their prey when the dogs reached them.

'Run! Run!'

The horses' hooves hammered on the ground.

Tu tump tu tump tu tump . . .

They came closer and closer . . . it was a noise which made Tommy's head throb.

How many were there? Ten, a hundred?

Tu tump tu tump tu tump . . .

'Run!'

They had reached the river bank.

'Into the water! So the dogs can't follow our tracks,' commanded Peg Leg Joe.

They slithered down, one at a time, moaning with fear.

Even if the Tombigbee was actually a stream not much bigger than the one where Tommy cast his fishing line, it was frightening because none of them knew how to swim.

They plunged into freezing water, up to their knees. The unstable river bottom was slimy and muddy, so they caught hold of roots and creepers growing along the banks to keep their balance, all the while clutching at their bundles, high above their heads.

'Keep low and walk,' Peg Leg Joe repeated.

The barking of the dogs was closer still.

'It's almost dawn,' said Papa, 'They'll see us.'

'Keep walking. We'll find shelter.'

'There's nothing here.'

'Yes there is,' said Peg Leg Joe.

The first ray of sun peeped out from behind the hills and struck them like a knife. The hooves of their pursuers' horses were closer still.

Jim Kniff's familiar voice rang out, 'Find them! Find them!'

'There!' said Peg Leg Joe pointing at something with a big hand.

Tommy was puzzled. What could he see that he couldn't?

He looked at an imposing willow tree: enormous and majestic, with its roots firmly anchored in the riverbank and a great crown which hung down low, brushing the water.

But it was only a tree.

Peg Leg Joe slipped under the willow's crown, they heard him climb onto the bank and grunt like a brown bear. He whistled softly to them to come, and helped them clamber up one at a time.

Hidden inside the crown of the tree was a grotto, quite big enough to hold them all, with a bed of fine dry sand onto which they all let themselves fall, soaked through and trembling.

'If you don't know it's here,' explained Peg Leg Joe, 'it's impossible to see. The dogs will lose our scent in the water. Now . . . be quiet and pray . . . there's nothing else we can do.'

They heard the hunters draw near and go up and down the riverbank.

They heard Jim Kniff's harsh, nasty voice, 'Find them, dammit! Find them! They are somewhere here, the dogs got their scent.'

The dogs growled, howled, scratched the ground like mad things as they hunted.

There was one terrifying moment when they glimpsed Jim Kniff through the willow's branches, standing stock still on the opposite bank of the Tombigbee, rifle in hand, dirty old hat pulled down over his forehead, staring straight in their direction.

Tommy felt his heart stop.

He was sure they could be seen, it was impossible not to be. He was sure that Jim Kniff was looking right at him. For one moment, he was tempted to get up, show himself and say, 'OK, I'm here, you've found me, please mister, please master, don't hurt me badly.'

But Jim Kniff didn't see them.

The noise of the horses hooves gradually died away and the barking of the dogs grew fainter, melting into silence.

Mamma began to cry. Tommy would gladly have done the same.

'For today,' said Peg Leg Joe, 'this will be your Station. There's no other. Don't let's fool ourselves: they won't give up the chase. I advise you,' he then added, turning to Papa, 'not to go out until it's totally dark.'

'You won't be here?' asked Papa.

'I have to go on ahead of you.'

'It's dangerous.'

'I know what I'm about.'

'But those dogs . . .'

'Always follow the direction of the river,' replied Peg Leg. 'Don't stray from it for any reason whatsoever. I'll leave you signs. Tommy knows how to recognise them. You remember?'

For a moment, Tommy couldn't remember a thing. He was tired, cold, and tremendously frightened. He was certain the hunters and Jim Kniff and the dogs would come back and find them.

Left foot,

peg foot . . .

the Guide sang softly.

. . . travelling on

finished Tommy.

'You see? You do still remember. The success of the mission depends on you.'

Peg Leg Joe cautiously stuck his head out from under the crown of the tree.

'It looks like the coast's clear.'

'When shall we see you again?' asked Papa.

'I'll find you.'

Peg Leg Joe let himself slide down into the water, managing, despite his bulk, not to make any noise. A second later, he was no longer there.

Jim Kniff told his men to dismount, tie up the dogs, make camp and treat themselves to a plug of tobacco.

Nothing else could be done. The runaways had gone to ground in a place where not even the dogs could unearth them.

Might as well make themselves comfortable. He was in no hurry.

They would come out at night, that much he knew.

He would wait. Those Negroes had no idea of where they were. They never know anything anyway.

He knew this territory, they didn't.

They could wander about aimlessly, if they were stupid enough to do so, but there were farms all around. Sooner or later someone would spot the runaways and shoot at them. No one wanted a group of lice-ridden Negroes roaming around their property. That afternoon he would send out the boys to warn the farm owners that there were slaves on the run.

Or they might stay clinging to the river's course like a tick on a mare's rump.It was the only reference point they had.

Yes sir. He bet on his new boots that's how it would go.

He would begin patrolling the area again once darkness fell. One way or another he would flush them out.

Jim Kniff made himself comfortable.

Nine

Cold. Darkness. Fear.

The river was even darker, slimier, muddier at night.

A pool as black as coal.

Impossible to see anything but blackness.

The one slice of the waning moon was covered by low, ragged clouds hurrying from one place to another, to discharge their rain.

Sludge. Water weeds wrapping around their legs. There were invisible creatures too. Tommy heard hissing, whispering, gurgling; the plop of something jumping into the water. At one point a chilly beating of immense wings brushed him behind the ears.

They stumbled on blindly, one behind the other, supporting one another, looking for some precarious handhold in the scrub on the bank.

They had to walk against the current. Little by little as they went forward, the water flowed faster, making their balance even more unsteady.

Tommy hung on to Papa, while Mamma hugged his sisters tightly, protecting them as a mother hen does her chicks. He was frightened and longed to say to his father, 'Hold me in your arms. Let's go back to our cabin. Papa, please, take me away from here.' Then he felt ashamed.

Peg Leg Joe had said he was counting on him to guide the group beyond the Tombigbee springs. He'd badly misplaced his trust.

Every so often, as soon as the riverbank sank lower, they would leave the water and climb up on to dry land where they could walk more easily – and fast. But then there'd be barking, or whinnying, or voices, making them hurry back down into the river to stay hidden under the bank, soaked through, to wait in silence.

They had spent an endless, anxious day in the little cave under the weeping willow, huddled together in the restricted space, feeling as though the walls would close in and they would suffocate. They had run out of food. But their pursuers had gone away.

Tommy had fallen asleep and woken up endless times to hear the hypnotic sound of the river running past. His dreams had been strange and confused.

When he reopened his eyes, he saw his father and Sammy on guard at the entrance to the cave, looking out through the crown of the willow to see if Jim Kniff and his men were coming back.

Tired and confused, they had left the shelter only when it was already pitch dark. They climbed up the bank into a tangle of reeds, ferns and shrubs where they would be invisible, though not to the dogs. They could rest for a few minutes in the dry. Sammy comforted Sarah, Mamma comforted Aretha and Daisy Mae . . . and him, who would comfort him? No one! Though there was Papa, but men don't do molly-coddling.

Tommy remembered his magic charm. He'd forgotten it in the heat of the chase. Rummaging anxiously in the pockets of his overalls, he wondered if he'd lost it. Had it slipped into the water?

But the lightning point was still there. Tommy felt it rough and comforting beneath his fingers. He squeezed it tight, and felt strong and brave.

Papa and Peg Leg Joe were counting on him to read the signs that would lead them to safety. He wouldn't disappoint them.

From now on, he would march at the head of the group, as expected. He would keep the Drinking Gourd always in sight to find the right path.

He glanced up at the sky. A gust of wind had swept the clouds away. The sickle moon shone out once more. Above him stretched the heavenly vault. All those stars!

The river too, just for a moment, began to gurgle in a friendly way.

He looked for the Drinking Gourd. There it was! And there was the brightest star showing him the way.

It was right in front of them: they were heading in the right direction.

He got up to tell Papa and Sammy who were conferring a little way off from the others, but there was rustling in the reeds behind him.

He turned, as did all the others, to see the reeds part, and stones scatter. Someone, or something – was it Jim Kniff, whip in hand? – was looming out of the darkness.

Nothing could be done. Nossir, there was nowhere to hide.

'Damn!' said Peg Leg Joe. 'What a time it's taken to find you!'

'What are you looking at me like that for? I've brought you something to eat . . . here!'

He shook open a leather bag closed carefully with a tie.

'What is it?' asked the boy.

'You'll see!'

'So they like playing Hide and Seek,' thought Jim Kniff, 'but I'll find them just the same.'

He was sure they were hiding along the river, but it was difficult to keep watch over both banks. In some parts the wood was thick and the ground uneven, and the water played havoc with the scent for the dogs. But they would turn up sooner or later, and he would be there, ready and waiting.

One of his men riding half a mile further down the valley yelled into the night, 'The dogs! The dogs!'

They had found the scent.

He dug his spurs into his horse's side.

The dogs were barking in the same direction, excited.

The pack hurled itself decisively through the scrub of undergrowth towards the river. The men left their mounts, took up their rifles, and followed on foot.

The Negroes were trapped.

Jim Kniff sniffed the wind; the hunt excited him too.

He knew very well what effect the sound of barking growing nearer could have on a man hidden in the darkness.

Hopeless.

The dogs broke down a cane thicket uncovering a little clearing and stopped.

'They're in there!'

They took the last stretch of bank running, sliding in the mud.

There was something odd, not quite right.

The dogs were barking madly.

They were trained, when they found their prey, to point at it barking and showing their teeth, until their master arrived. But they would not howl and attack without a command.

'A torch!' ordered Jim.

He went into the clearing holding a flaming resinous branch above his head.

There was nobody there.

The dogs spun around on themselves, yelping and rubbing their muzzles in the thin grass.

Jim Kniff got down on his knees, rubbed his hand over the ground, then sniffed at it, and sneezed vigorously. Someone had sprayed black pepper all over the ground.

He swore.

An entire pack of dogs was out of action. For that day, the hunt was ended.

He could go back to the estate and get others, but doing that would give the runaways an entire day's advantage, and it would be even harder to pick up the scent again.

What gnawed at him more than anything was something else: those Negroes had tricked him. Damn! They'd fooled him!

He knew Negroes well. A joke like that could never have entered the head of one of them. They were animals, in essence, like oxen pulling a plough in the fields, or mules attached to cart shafts; they could be likeable and playful like puppies, or snarling and treacherous as a jackal.

A Negro didn't have the courage, or imagination, to organise a group of runaways.

Every so often a Negro escaped, but they were isolated cases. Unfortunately there would always be one hothead, there was always a rotten apple: one who nurtured bitterness and hate and didn't appreciate all that the white masters were doing for him. They didn't know where to go and were always caught.

But this time it was different. The escape had been organised; planned.

Jim Kniff energetically scratched his head. Who was he dealing with?

Who could have thought up that delaying tactic of scattering pepper?

Worst of all, he bet his bottom dollar the story would get out.

Of course he'd threaten his men that he'd cut out the tongue of the first one who let a single word slip about what had happened that night. He'd tell them he'd flay with his own hands the first one who, in exchange for a whisky or two, would lower his voice at the counter of some bar to tell how that fool Jim Kniff, yes, him from The Oaks, had been fooled by a bunch of Negroes.

It would get out. At The Oaks. At the Emporium. At Jackson's shop, the barber's where he went to have a bath in the tub out the back once a month. In the dives and in the saloons within a radius of forty miles. Across half Alabama.

They would hear Jim Kniff had been fooled by a Negro!

Oh, how they'd laugh!

As he ordered his men to keep those blasted dogs quiet, by kicking them if necessary, and was turning back to look for his horse, another thought struck him with the violence of a drunken Saturday night. What if the other Negroes on the plantation knew too?

He stopped dead in his tracks.

Somehow, they always managed to know everything. It was as if they had a telegraph which kept them informed, a secret code.

A Negro thing, in fact.

And then, first of all, he'd have to tell Captain Archer.

Captain, I let them get away.

A very bad day indeed.

Ten

The next few nights they marched on, following the banks of the Tombigbee, hearts in mouths and ears pricked to catch the slightest sound above the gurgling of the river which accompanied them.

Several times they thought they heard galloping hooves pounding the earth; the neighing of a nervous horse; angry male voices carried on the wind, but they couldn't say for certain that they were their pursuers. Each time they hurried to a precarious refuge.

Now and again the river was lost in broad meanders, or got bogged down in thickets of reeds, or they had to abandon it and seek another route which was longer and more tortuous because of some farmhouse nearby, and the danger of being seen was too great.

Each time, Tommy explained that all they had to do was look for the Drinking Gourd high up above, in the immensity of the starry heavens. That way the right road could be found. If the river forked, or lost itself in myriad streams and they lost track of the main current, Tommy went on ahead to spy out the land. On the bank, Peg Leg Joe's sign marked a dead tree.

By night, skirting tilled fields, Papa and Sammy found something to get their teeth into: corncobs, sweet potatoes, or a pepper. They would run like the wind if some guard dog did his duty.

It was stealing, granted, but they had empty stomachs and had no choice as Papa explained to Tommy. So it wasn't a serious crime. In fact, it was God providing for them.

'Sure?' asked Tommy.

'Sure enough,' replied Papa.

Tommy would have liked to cast his fishing line into the Tombigbee, even without his favourite worms to use as bait, and put his skill as a fisherman to the test. He was sure he'd manage to catch a tasty supper for everyone.

But lighting a fire was strictly forbidden, for safety reasons, and despite their hunger, eating raw fish did not appeal.

Then, one moonless night, Sammy came back from one of his raids with a chicken under his arm and an old asthmatic dog barking at his heels.

Sammy was faster, and the old dog gave up, out of breath, and looked miserable as he went off. In the good old days he wouldn't have let a chicken thief get away like that. He'd caught so many!

Sammy showed the others his booty and their eyes shone with happiness.

They went off at a run, while the chicken clucked and shed feathers, found a sheltered bend in the river, far from roads and farmhouses, and collapsed onto a little beach of fine dry sand.

'We need something warming,' said Mamma. 'All of us. Look for wood and light a fire.'

'You know it's not wise to do that,' said Papa anxiously.

'We'll eat the chicken and drink the broth if it's the last thing we do,' said Mamma decisively. 'The children need it.'

Everyone nodded vigorously.

'The lady's right,' said Peg Leg Joe. 'Let's take the risk. We need all our strength.'

A few minutes later, a good fire was crackling for the first time they could remember since leaving the plantation. How many days had it been since they began their escape? Three days, or three weeks, or three months? Not, three months, surely?

Yet it was a heap of time. Only a few days though. They couldn't agree on it.

They spent the next hour sitting in a circle around the fire staring at the pot in which the chicken was boiling, as if they could miraculously speed up the cooking.

No one spoke. The only sounds were the bubbling in the pot, the gurgling river, the grumbling of eight empty stomachs.

When the scent of the broth began to mix with the river mist, Tommy thought he would go mad. He imagined the smell wafting along the whole river, reaching into the valley and beyond. It would be an irresistible summons. Following its trail, people would swarm in from everywhere to gobble up their chicken. There wouldn't be a single piece left for him. At this thought, his stomach tied itself in even more knots. The asthmatic old dog would come too, and eat up the bones.

'It's ready!' announced Mamma.

What a tremendous feast!

Since it was only a few hours until dawn, they decided not to start walking again that night, they could take it easy – for once! – and would stay stretched out on that soft sand listening to the river, chatting, having a nap, and get their tired bones in working order again.

Jim Kniff and his dogs could go to the devil.

He probably wasn't even looking for them anymore.

'They're still looking for us,' announced Peg Leg Joe. He came and went continually, staying with them for a couple of days, then disappearing again. Each time he managed to find them as if he were guided by a sixth sense.

He, Papa and Tommy were on the upper floor of an old hay barn which was the Station sheltering them that day. Through the little windows and the cracks between the beams, they could survey the land round about. On one side there was deep shade at the edge of the wood, on the other they could scan carefully tended square fields extending to the banks of the river, together with orchards and cornfields descending to the valley.

There was a great silence and peacefulness in the air, broken only by animals lowing in the stable and the rhythmic sound of a hammer on metal, carried by the wind, as if somewhere, far away, a blacksmith was dealing with a horse needing to be shoed.

As usual, they wouldn't have known whose farm it was which was sheltering them. As usual, no one would wander around the hay barn, though caution made them take turns guarding, while the others slept heavily in the middle of hay bales on the floor below.

'They're still looking for us,' explained Peg Leg Joe. 'Captain Archer has had posters printed and they've stuck them up everywhere.'

'Posters?'

'Yep! Seen them with my own eyes. Can't miss them. There's not a street corner, or telegraph pole, or low dive around here where there isn't one. Yeah, you can be sure of it. They've even nailed them to trees. They would've stuck them to cows' rumps if they could. But the cows are good beasts. D'you know what's written in black and white, ink on paper? They've written we're runaway slaves. Say we're thieves and assassins. Yes sir. There's one hundred dollars in gold for whoever catches us and takes us to Jim Kniff. One hundred dollars in gold! With bounty money like that, a man from round here wouldn't get rich, but he could buy a little herd and settle down.

'*Oh yes*. Anyone in the whole county will be ready to sell us for that, you can bet on it. They'll all have their eyes wide open, they'll be examining the ground in search of tracks, sniffing the air for the scent of Negro, they'll run to the sheriff to report the disappearance of a shirt hung out to dry. "I'm sure it was them, sheriff," they'll say. "Only a Negro on the run would steal an old holey shirt. And if you remember the bounty, sheriff, remember it was me who found them!" That's what they'll say, you can bet on it.'

Tommy's eyes were as big as the frying pan in which Mamma used to fry the bacon at home – when there was any.

'You know how to read?' he asked.

Peg Leg Joe downplayed it, 'A bit.'

Tommy's mouth fell open.

A Negro who could read had never been seen nor heard of. But then a Negro who was not a slave had never been seen nor heard of either. And maybe . . .

'Do you know how to write?' Tommy asked hesitantly.

'A bit,' Peg Leg Joe downplayed it again.

Tommy was so astonished that he barely heard the rest of the speech.

'In two days,' said Peg Leg Joe, 'you'll reach the springs of the Tombigbee and climb the mountain Tommy knows how to recognise. You'll find another river, a bigger one, to give you the direction. You'll no longer be in Alabama, but watch out, the danger will be no less than now.

'We'll still be surrounded by enemies. But you'll have completed the first part of the journey, even if what remains is longer and harder. But you'll have done it and succeeded. How d'you feel?'

'The women are tired,' said Papa.

'They'll make it,' replied Peg Leg Joe. 'You'll see. They're stronger than us.'

'You must be kidding!' protested Tommy.

'You don't know much about anything. One of these days I'll tell you about Harriet, remind me.'

'Who's Harriet?'

'She's an extraordinary woman, she really is. You remember the song I sang, the evening I arrived at your village?'

'Which one?' asked Tommy.

Peg Leg Joe hummed under his breath:

Dark and thorny is the pathway
Where the pilgrim makes his way

Of course! Tommy knew it by heart.

But beyond dis vale of sorrow
Lie the fields of endless days.

'Exactly right. Well it was Harriet who wrote it. There's not a plantation in the United States; not a field, or stable, or shop . . . not a sawmill in the woods, or anywhere a bellows blows on fire, or a hammer beats on an anvil raising sparks like in hell, or echoes against hard stones in a quarry beneath the sun . . . there's not a pigsty, or a smoky kitchen with servants bustling at night to prepare the master's breakfast . . . there's not a place under the sun in the South where slaves labour . . . that don't sing or know Harriet's song. The heart of the person who knows its real meaning swells and he thinks, "One day all this will end." Harriet Tubman, little man, remember that name. Respect.'

'Tell me the story now!' begged Tommy.

'*Naaaah*. It's not the right time. I have to go. For the next two days you're the Guide, got that? Where does the river end?'

'Between two hills,' replied Tommy quickly.

'And what's on the other side?'

'Another river,' came the answer.

'*Yeaahhh!*' approved Peg Leg Joe.

A moment later he was gone.

Tommy couldn't sleep. He tossed and turned and thought about that mysterious woman, Harriet, who had dreamed about fields of endless days.

He didn't know what they were, but he knew that it was there he wanted to be.

Were the fields of endless days the thing they called freedom?

Eleven

The swamp was cold, dark, silent. For two days they walked immersed up to their knees in murky water, slowly, one step after another, in a tangle of mud, water weeds, gigantic tree roots so tall as to hide the sky. They were tormented by mosquitoes and swarms of insects.

The only sound was the thump of water creatures and the cry of mysterious birds that remained invisible, hidden in the dense foliage.

The swamp was dead.

It was all the same wherever you looked, no reference points, no way of orientating yourself because the sky, covered by a layer of cloud and mist, glimmered only a vague brightness which stayed the same from dawn to dusk. No sun, no starry night vault, no Drinking Gourd to follow.

Perhaps they were going straight, or in the wrong direction, or round in circles like the spokes on a wheel, always returning to the same place.

They were lost.

There must have been everything in that swamp, and deadly water moccasin snakes whose bite was lethal. It would take two minutes, even less, for the strongest of men to die in unimaginable suffering – or so they had heard.

Papa had given out sturdy sticks to the men. At every step they be at the stagnant water to keep the snakes away.

But there had to be something else, Tommy was certain, he felt it: the souls of the unhappy dead, grey souls, cold like that desolate place, intangible as the wreaths of mist hanging on the black twisted branches. Souls that wanted to hold them in this swamp forever.

He seemed to see them moving alongside, stretching out spidery arms in an attempt to grab hold of them, and then disappear, mingling with the horizon which blurred water and sky; air and spirit.

Tommy clutched the lightning point in his hand and walked, one step after another, smacking the water round him, lifting his feet with difficulty because of the mud's imprisoning grip which sucked them in.

There were so many things that might emerge from beneath that slimy, putrid, stagnant water. He knew the earth spirits and the ones at the crossroads, the ones from the cemetery and how to avoid them. But that swamp was not of this world. Anything could have been born in that ancient mud, beneath the prehistoric filth. From one minute to the next an arm, a hoof, a thing . . . armed with cruel claws . . . could emerge from the depths to grab hold of him by the neck and pull him under. Tommy beat the water around him harder.

Even Peg Leg Joe seemed to be having a hard time, which frightened the boy most of all. He saw how his wooden leg made climbing difficult, how he moved back and forth continuously seeking reference points, how he sniffed the air and searched for any sign on the tree bark.

Moss was everywhere and there were no signs.

'Let's stop here,' said Peg Leg Joe.

Every now and again the swamp was broken up by stretches of solid ground, usually little islands formed by the roots of aquatic trees, and by silt deposited by the water. Just now they were facing one which was particularly big, capable of holding them all.

At least they would be dry for a few hours and it was easier to keep an eye out for snakes. They hauled themselves up onto the little island and sank to the ground, while Papa and Sammy collected some branches that seemed a bit less wet than others and tried to light a fire.

The flint and steel always travelled safely in the dry place inside Sammy's cap which he never took off, even when he slept.

The wood crackled, spat, seemed to go out, but came alive as a miserable little fire which produced more smoke than heat. They stayed round it to gaze into the dancing flames and try and warm their bones.

They did not know if it was morning or afternoon. In the swamp the pale transparent light never changed. Only suddenly, darkness would fall.

Tommy dreaded yet another night in the absolute darkness of this deadly place that not even the light of the fire could affect. He thought about the odd noises and voices that seemed to fill the swamp at night and whisper in the ears of the lost people.

They had nothing to eat.

Tommy dozed off.

In the days before, they had finally arrived at the mountain with two peaks – what was it called? – and they had climbed it. On the other side there was a new river, exactly like the song said. A big, wide, real river which ran north and they had followed it night after night.

What was that river called?

Tennessee.

And the territory they were crossing was also called Tennessee, Peg Leg Joe had explained.

It was wild land and largely unpopulated. They walked for days on end without seeing a farm or a cabin, only the endless expanse of meadow grass where the wind whistled and the clouds raced towards the vast horizon. The air was pure and clear. There were occasional thick dark forests with fallow deer jumping the ravines, or wild pigs running around in the undergrowth, or water from streams cascading into the valley.

There was no risk of being seen and denounced, but still they struggled, as there were no roads, or paths; nothing to show the way. They lost time, whole days even, because of complicated diversions when there was an insurmountable obstacle like a stream in full spate, impossible to ford, or a mountain too difficult to climb. Despite Peg Leg Joe's cleverness and expertise, they went round in a circle.

There was no grapevine telegraph so it was hard to find food. They ate wild berries and fruit, grubs, grasses, and roots. Mamma boiled up everything in her saucepan, but most of the time their empty stomachs ached as they walked.

Sammy wove traps with a special long leaf that was tough and flexible, and prepared traps for wild rabbits, but he rarely caught one.

They were tired, their feet sore with blisters, shoes falling apart and no possibility of replacing them.

Their reference point was the big river. When they could follow its course more closely it became easier to find food and shelter. They began to come across Stations: seemingly deserted farms, or haystacks, or cowsheds where even the oxen had orders not to see them and pretend nothing was happening. Or there were simple cabins where slaves like themselves risked their lives to help them. At times they sheltered in the soft furrows of a ploughed field, and there were often mysterious figures, strangers, apparently doing nothing stretched out in the shade of a tree, pretending to sleep, ready to raise the alarm in the event of danger.

'Who are they?'

'Friends, they've been informed by the grapevine telegraph.'

Then they had had to abandon the river and make a long detour – days and days of walking – to avoid a town. Tommy forgot its name. Too many people, too many streets, too many carts, too dangerous.

'We'll pick up the river again further north,' said Peg Leg Joe.

They had seen a train of six mule-driven carts coming at them along the track, accompanied by a cloud of red dust, and fled fast.

'They gave me a turn, Slim, did you see them?'

'What?'

'A bunch of Negroes. Stinking Negroes. They slunk off that way.'

'So? There's lots of Negroes around here.'

'There's Negroes everywhere, but they gave me a turn.'

'So? '

'I don't like the ones who slink off.'

'Negroes are always slinking off. How long to the stable?'

'A couple of hours.'

'I want a whisky. And bed.'

'A whisky will do me.'

'They must've lost their way and finished up in the swamp.'

Tommy woke up with a start.

He sat up rubbing his eyes. The fire burned weakly in a cloud of smoke that made him cough. He didn't know if ten minutes or ten hours had gone by. The usual soft whiteish light spread over the swamp. Invisible birds chirped hidden in the branches.

There was a new, sloshing sound. Perhaps that is what had woken him, even though it was not loud.

It was the sound of an oar breaking the surface of the water.

Tommy looked up and saw the man gliding towards them like a ghost. He emerged from the mist which wreathed the edges of the swamp. Perhaps he was the soul of an unhappy spirit. Was he coming to bring comfort, or to ask for it?

The others sat up, holding their breath. Mamma murmured a prayer, or a charm.

The canoe came at them.

The man paddling had dark skin, but he was definitely not a Negro. He was bearded, dressed in rough clothes made out of skins, and on his head he had a hat of opossum fur; a big knife strapped at his waist and a rifle slung over his shoulder.

He stopped a few metres from them.

No one spoke.

The man looked at them for a long time, every now and again giving a little touch with the paddle to keep the canoe upright.

Who knows what impression they made on him: they were threadbare, ragged, and had plastered their faces, necks, chest and any exposed part of their bodies with green mud in an attempt to keep off the insects.

Perhaps they looked like ghosts to him too.

A marten plopped into the water.

Out of the corner of his eye, Tommy noticed a fat leech climbing up the bank and thought he had better be careful. Leeches were bad.

The man turned the canoe, paddled slowly to a fork, and stopped.

Papa and Peg Leg Joe looked at each other, then at the man.

'Let's go.' For two hours, everyone waded in the water behind the canoe that led the way. Finally the man stopped. Using an oar, he pointed to a long channel to one side. It was almost overgrown with vegetation. He went off in the opposite direction, without uttering a word.

They emerged from the swamp at sunset.

A pale washed-out sun was sinking behind arid hills. It was a miraculous sight. They collapsed in a field of dry grass and fell asleep beneath a great flight of crows in the sky.

Twelve

'Harriet,' said Peg Leg Joe. 'You want me to tell you about Harriet.'

'You promised,' insisted Tommy.

Peg Leg Joe took another roasted corncob and swiftly ground it up in his great teeth.

They were camped on the bank of a stream, in an isolated place away from prying eyes. The sun shone bright, the air was fresh and clean, centuries-old oak trees marked out the line of the horizon. The sound was that of insects buzzing and birds singing.

They had rested and cleaned themselves up. They had washed their threadbare clothes, beating them for a long time against the flat, smooth stones of the shore. In the abandoned field around what had once been a farm, its roof fallen in and walls covered in ivy and creepers, they had found corncobs and apples which had not gone completely wild, and dug up sweet potatoes.

Tommy had demonstrated his skill as a fisherman, and the stream had been generous.

It was a good piece of land. And peaceful. A place where a man would want to stop and put down roots – be he black, or white. All he'd need was a hoe, a plough, an old nag.

But they could not stop, because they were Negroes, therefore slaves.

They could not stop because any bounty hunter would shoot them, hammer a chain around their ankles and drag them to the nearest sheriff to collect one hundred dollars in gold. That was their job.

Or it might be some clever, honest, pious white man who on seeing them would feel shaken to the core and be indignant. Negroes! Free! Such a thing ran against nature, the law and God's will. And what if they'd taken a piece of land too?! Something like that could not possibly be allowed to happen. That evening he would look seriously at his honest and pious wife, would place his hands solemnly on the fine white linen tablecloth on each side of his plate and say to her, 'It is my duty to denounce them.' She would nod, trembling at the mere thought of how much her husband would be risking in denouncing Negro slaves. Thoughts and preoccupations.

A brave man, a just man. The next morning he would present himself at the sheriff's office, best hat in hand, a gold chain across his waistcoat. 'Sheriff . . .'

'Harriet,' Peg Leg Joe said again.

The runaways surrounded him. Some were stretched out, some with their feet soaking in the fresh water of the stream. They were full, at peace for once. It was the right time to listen to a story.

Harriet wasn't always called Harriet, he began. 'No sir. Before, she was called Aramitha.'

'Before what?'

'"Before . . . Do you know who Aramitha was?'

'No.'

'She was a slave, a black bum, excuse my language, like me and like you Sammy, like Tommy and like all of you.

An object. An animal. She was the property of the Thompsons, down Maryland way.'

'Where's Maryland?' Tommy wanted to know.

'Stop interrupting me. Maryland's somewhere over there,' and he gestured.

'Sure?'

'No. Aramitha was only five years old, but she already had to look after the mistress's newborn baby girl. Bah, it wasn't like playing with dolls. If the little one woke during the night and cried, disturbing the master's peace, Aramitha was whipped. So every night Aramitha would sit on a little stool alongside the cradle and rock it – *rockabye . . . rockabye . . .* – and would watch, eyes open wide, that marvel of white lace, ribbons and laces, the little bell jingling at every movement, and the little embroidered sheet. The baby would look at her and laugh. Then Aramitha would fall asleep and crying would suddenly wake her, *rockabye . . . rockabye . . .* before the mistress woke up. She would have liked to sing a little song to this tiny, delicate creature, a little song to make her dream sweet dreams so she wouldn't wake up during the night. But she didn't know any little songs, her mother had never had time to let her hear them, she worked hard, her mamma, and had nine children. Aramitha didn't have sweet dreams either, I bet.'

'Mamma sometimes sang little songs to us,' chorused Aretha and Daisy Mae. 'There was one which went . . . '

'They sold them all. Brothers, sisters. Every so often she would get up in the morning and Bess wasn't there any more. Or Isaiah. Or little Will whom she'd played with the night before. It was useless asking where they were, or when they would come back. They had been sold, just as if they were animals from a stable. Finally, she was the only one left. She was thirteen when that white man hit her on the head, down at the shop in Calumet. It was late morning. Aramitha was looking through the window at the dust from the street which was making little whirlpools and irritating a horse in the shafts. Perhaps she was day-dreaming, perhaps she was enjoying the smell of molasses and carob in the old shop, or the freshness of the twilight. They said the white man was a farmhand from the Mulligan farm. He took an iron weight, one of those they use on scales, one of the big ones.'

'Why in God's name?' asked Mamma.

'Who knows. She lay in the sawdust for three hours, blood pouring out, then they loaded her onto a cart and took her back to the Thompsons, to the farm. It looked like she was dying and or if not she'd be soft in the head. Every now and again her eyes rolled back, so you could see the whites, and she'd fall to the ground trembling all over. I saw her once. It happened right in front of me. Oh man. She really gave me a fright, believe me. She'd have visions. Say things.'

'What would she say?'

'No one understood.'

'But did you know her, Peg Leg Joe? Really?'

'Ah, Harriet . . .'

Peg Leg Joe scratched his big head. Dust, sawdust, leaves, a variety of seeds, a little beetle rained down.

'What was wrong with her? Why was she like that?'

'Who knows. Not even the wise women understood it. One said that she had *grand mal*, but what that mysterious illness was, no one knew. Do you want to know what I think? '

'Yes.'

'She was just fooling them. All of them. She was tricking them. Her masters, the white people. The Thompsons wanted to sell her, but who'd want a feeble-minded slave possessed by devils? Every time a prospective buyer came, Aramitha would have a crisis, faint, go mad. Or she'd pretend to fall into a very deep sleep from which it was impossible to wake her. A sleep like death. They'd take to their heels.'

'Did she really carry on like that?' Papa asked admiringly.

'You bet she did. The Thompsons had to keep her and they didn't trust themselves to make her do anything. But I can imagine the rage. Aramitha would go raving about the farm and as soon as she could would escape to listen to the preachers and learn stories from the Bible. She learned the story of Moses by heart. How he led the Hebrews, who were slaves hunted by the Pharaoh and his men, out of Egypt, and guided them to the Promised Land where they were free.'

'Like us?' asked Tommy.

'Oh yes, man. And then they married her off to John Tubman who was a freed slave and a good-hearted man, but he couldn't really keep her, Aramitha.'

'No?'

'Naaaahhhh! She'd made her choice. One night when there was a full moon – it was September and the first autumn winds were shaking the bushes and you could hear owls hooting in the branches of the big oak tree. Aramitha became Harriet, like a snake changing its skin. She put two handfuls of yellow flour and a piece of bacon in a shoulder bag, slipped a revolver and six bullets under her skirt, and escaped. What a woman, children! A she-devil.'

Mamma, Sammy's silent young wife, and the girls listened in disbelief.

'A revolver?' murmured Mamma.

'Yeahhhh, ma'am!'

'She managed to escape?'

'She got as far as Pennsylvania.'

'Where's Pennsylvania?' asked Tommy.

'Don't keep interrupting me. It's somewhere over there, where we're going too. More or less.'

'And then?'

'There she found someone who helped her and was free. She also knew some important people who told her that slavery is an affront to God. They founded an organisation. And you know what Harriet did? She became a Guide.'

'Like you!'

'Harriet was the first Guide. Every year Harriet returns to Maryland and takes a group of slaves across America to safety. She's already done it six times and run a thousand risks. Every white man in the South is looking for her, every sheriff, all the bounty hunters. Just hearing her name makes the veins on their necks stand out, the beer go down the wrong way, and they foam at the mouth with rage. A woman! A Negro woman who's always getting the better of them. Making them mad with rage. We're worth a hundred dollars in gold as I've told you. Well, Harriet alone is worth a thousand. Do you know how many posters they've printed with her name and description? In every village in the South there are more posters about Harriet than fleas on a stray dog's back. You can go whistle for her. She knows all the tricks, all the dodges. And she says, "I've always got six bullets under my skirt." And she really would fire them, you better believe it.'

Tommy, like the others, was listening open-mouthed. He swallowed two flies.

'And she's written that song . . .'

'It's like a word of command. A signal. A warning to be ready. She's brought the grapevine telegraph everywhere. There's not a slave cabin even in the furthest away, remote place . . . there's not a Negro, no matter how rough and ignorant . . . there's not a woman, her back breaking under the sun in a cotton row, who doesn't know by now that if someone sings "Dark and thorny is the pathway", then the door to hope opens up for you too. Brother, if you want, you can be free.'

'Like you did in our village.'

'Exactly. Do you know what they call Harriet? "The Black Moses", they call her, the Moses for her race. And she's exactly that.'

Everyone stayed silent for a few minutes.

'And you,' Papa wanted to know, 'how did you know her?'

'After her first journey, Harriet taught other Guides. One of them freed me and taught me. Every Guide tries to teach another one. It's the only way the organisation can stay alive.'

'Is it difficult to become a Guide?' asked Tommy, pre-tending to be indifferent.

'Very difficult. It takes courage. Heart and brain. You need to learn lots of things. To read. To write. To play the banjo. To find your way.

'To pretend. To sniff the wind and rain. To disguise yourself. To become a wolf and a snake. So many things.

But above all you need to learn one thing without which all the others are worthless.'

'What?'

'That freedom is worth more than your life. Other people's freedom too. Man, don't think it's easy. It's not easy at all. You have doubts every day. Just think, you're sitting under an oak tree waiting for the rain to stop, more alone than a coyote, and you don't exactly know where you are, except it's somewhere between Arkansas and the Mississippi. It's like being nowhere. It's all the same. Or you're in bed in Philadelphia, in your little den, when you hear noises down below in the street of the city waking, and you've already prepared your bag with two things which you must always carry. You know that same night you'll leave on another journey.Then you think, "Why does it have to be me?"'

'Why indeed?' asked Papa.

'Man!' said Peg Leg Joe. 'How can I answer that? I don't know how to make clever speeches. I'm a simple man. I think about all those suffering in chains. About all those who will feel the whip tomorrow. Then I take my bag and go.'

'Aren't you scared?' asked Tommy.

'The whole time, yes, you can depend on it.'

'But then . . .'

'Then nothing. You know what Harriet says? She says, "I've never left anyone behind. Write it on my grave when the time comes – 'I have never left anyone behind'".'

Peg Leg Joe got up and stretched noisily, yawning wide enough to dislocate his jaw. 'On we go.'

When he spoke in a certain tone there was no discussion.

Thirteen

Days blurred into one another.

Despite exhaustion, blisters on his feet, hunger and fear, Tommy began to love their journey: he was seeing new things, learning new things. The countryside was always different too and the weather gradually changed as they pushed north. The air became fresher, especially in the evening, and the days grew shorter. The trees began to have red leaves. Above all, Tommy enjoyed being able to spend a lot of time with Peg Leg Joe.

During the night time marches, in free moments during the breaks, in that ambiguous hour which was not day or night, as they set up camp in the open, or in one of the Stations which someone had prepared for them, Tommy was always with the Guide. He followed him like a shadow.

He never tired of talking to Peg Leg Joe, of interrogating him, asking him questions, listening to his stories. Peg Leg Joe was brave, strong and decisive. He always knew how to get by. It wasn't by accident that everyone turned to him for anything, it was logical.

When he went on ahead to prepare their next stopover, everyone felt his absence. 'When will Joe be back?'

He had travelled, had seen unimaginable things, and people.He had lived in big cities like Philadelphia, which was much bigger than anything they could imagine.

Although Tommy loved his Papa very much, he would have liked to have a Papa like Peg Leg Joe. His father was a good man, a generous man who had never slapped him – or maybe just once as he'd deserved it – and told him off only when it was necessary.

Tommy knew, from talking to the other children in the village back on Captain Archer's plantation, that not all Papas were like that. He knew that some of them came back from the cotton fields so tired and worn out that they had neither the time nor the will to do anything. They never talked, but went and hid in the back of their cabin to unearth a bottle of the most horrible bootleg brandy which would burn throat and soul a bit at a time. He knew that there were some whom the whip and chains had made wicked and violent, and every so often, a child would come for shelter in their cabin where, huddled in a corner to sleep, he could be heard crying. Tommy knew all those things very well.

His father was always ready to talk to him, even when he was tired and sweat ran down his face dirty from the earth from the fields. But he got no joy out of talking to Papa, who would listen, certainly, and would inevitably say, 'You must be patient.' He would say, 'We're ignorant and can't understand these things.' And then he didn't have any stories to tell. And then . . .

As for his sisters, Tommy didn't like them one little bit. They only knew how to whine and complain. All they wanted was a white muslin dress for Sundays. That's if they did get somewhere and there'd be an opportunity to go to church.

And as for Sammy . . . good heavens! He was good and likeable and always smiling, but you never knew what to talk about with him. Sammy knew nothing, as he had spent his whole life picking cotton since he was six. When he tried to say anything, he stumbled over his words, got mixed up, burst out laughing, and gave up.

Tommy knew that wasn't his fault. And it wasn't his sisters' fault either, much less his Papa's. What fault could Papa have? He knew that he had to spend time with them 'cause they were his family. But still . . .

Tommy wanted something else, and he doubted that a family like his could understand what that was. On the other hand, Peg Leg Joe did.

Tommy felt mean and wicked having these thoughts, but they came to him just the same. He became quieter and quieter. Not even Mamma could break his stubborn silence.

'No, I'm fine,' was all he would say. He flitted around Peg Leg Joe like a moth about a flame.

They had to make a long detour, losing a heap of time, in order to avoid an area that was dangerous. They endured three days of a terrible march across a desolate stony place where they couldn't even find water. One by one they became shoeless, and wrapped rags around their feet to stop them bleeding. But walking became increasingly difficult and painful. They made slow progress, and were tired and discouraged.

Canaan, or Canada, or wherever they were going was like a mirage. Who knew where the place was. Did it even exist? Maybe it was only an invention, or an illusion; a fairy story for Negroes who are said to be credulous and will believe anything.

'There's a good Station within two days walking,' encouraged the Guide. 'One of the best places. I use it every journey.

We'll stop, rest, eat 'til we're full. They'll get us clothes and shoes and . . .'

Yes, maybe.

They camped in the middle of a clump of scrubby trees.

It was drizzling. A slow drizzle which penetrated everywhere.

Ahead of them, as far as the eye could see, the plain stretched out flat, grey, monotonous, a sea flattened by the howling wind.

They lit a cheerless fire and Mamma began boiling up some leftovers.

It was getting cold.

Way off in the evening half light, indistinct in the mist and rain, some hazy black shapes slowly came towards them across the prairie.

The runaways didn't even try to escape. There was no place to take cover. So they waited.

The strangers' slowness seemed ancient, primeval, as the night darkness moved behind them on the infinite prairie hiding it from sight like a cloak. The clouds raced towards the horizon.

Tommy felt as though they were alone in the middle of the world, even if he didn't know much about it. He looked at the wind, the clouds, the fading daylight, and the strange shapes coming at them – his heart beat fast.

'Who are they?' asked Papa.

'I don't know,' replied Peg Leg Joe.

Finally, they could make them out: seven men, three boys, four women with babies were walking in columns, and two horses pulled a sledge.

They arrived at the edge of the clump of trees sticking up from the prairie like an island in the sea, and halted wordlessly, as the last rays of light dissolved on the horizon.

None of the runaways had ever seen a redskin: there were no more Indians where the whites had arrived earlier and fenced in the land creating plantations and farms, building houses, cities and railways. They had been exterminated.

But everyone had heard of them. Was there anyone who hadn't listened at one time or another to one of Jim Kniff's stories, when after a couple of glasses he'd boast about his exploits in the wars against the Indians, fought under Captain Archer? How many he'd scalped!

Now they were there in front of them, at the edge of the circle of flickering light cast by the flames of the fire. They seemed more worn out and tired and ragged than they were. Old horse blankets were draped over shoulders as a protection from rain. Their moccasins were in no better shape than Tommy's shoes.

Papa and Sammy threw an armful of wood on the fire and the flames crackled into life. They signalled for the strangers to come forward and sit down.

A young man and an elder came and sat with legs crossed; the palms of their hands resting on their knees. The face of the old man in the firelight was like the bark of a sycamore; he was one with that cracked land engraved with canyons and plateaux and flowing rivers. A feather was stuck into the turquoise band around his head.

'We have no food,' said Peg Leg Joe quietly.

'Ah,' said the young man. 'Nor us.' He was little more than a boy and had a sad, gentle look. He didn't seem like a warrior.

'Are you the chief?' Peg Leg Joe asked the old man who was listening to the fire.

'He is *sakem*,' said the young man. 'But he has decided not to speak the white man's language any more. He only speaks *Shawnee*. I can speak.'

'Where are you going?'

'Away,' and the young man made a sweeping gesture with his arm towards the East.

'There is a place for us that the white man calls a "reservation". It's far away. We must go there.'

Tommy couldn't manage to restrain himself, even if he knew that he shouldn't interrupt adults, 'But why?'

The young man who did not look much older than him looked surprised, then smiled, 'Oh, Little Black Wolf. Do you want to know why? Look.'

He pointed to the circle of people behind him who were waiting at the edge of the camp. One of the horses pawed the ground.

'They are what is left of my tribe. We still have three children. The white men have taken our land. They're taking all the land of the Nation of Men.'

The old man began to speak and addressed no one in particular. Perhaps he was talking to himself, or to the wind, or to someone whom only he could see.

He spoke without moving his lips.

It was a lullaby, a dirge, a song.

The other remaining members of the tribe sat down to listen to the *sakem* too, but stayed outside the circle of the fire. The old man was telling a story.

For a few long moments, Tommy was absolutely sure that he understood what the old man was saying, even if he was speaking in a strange language. He could understand it in the same way – as a baby, at the beginning of his life – that he understood the song of the birds, or the language of the wolves who came up close to the edge of the village of cabins at dusk.

'This was the land of the *Shawnee* and the fathers of the *Shawnee* and the fathers of the fathers of the *Shawnee* and the *Shawnee* rode it in freedom, they set up their tents and were happy because all this was fair', sang the old man.

'Then the white man came,' the young man translated, 'and said that the land was his and the fruits of the land was his, as were the herds and the birds in the sky. They built fences in place of the wind. At that time the leader of the *Shawnee* was Chief Tecumseh and I was still strong and proud. Chief Tecumseh knew the white men, he'd wanted to study in their schools, to help his people. He said that the white men had no right to our lands which belonged to the *Shawnee* by nature's right which made us sovereign on our lands. Chief Tecumseh had learned these things in the white men's schools because they were written in the white men's books. They were written in the laws of the white men. Chief Tecumseh knew those laws. He met the head of the white men and told him these things. It was no use. Every day the white men wanted something more. They are greedy. Then Chief Tecumseh rode for six days and assembled the whole *Shawnee* tribe. In the morning at dawn, before the battle, he gave me the Chief's feather because he said he would join the

Great Spirit, and only I would survive. And so it was. That night, after the battle, with two frightened boys, we went back to look for his body in the darkness and the blood and the horses moaning. We carried it and buried it in the hollow trunk of a sacred oak tree so that at least his body would not be profaned by the white men. Only I am left, who knows where he lies.'

Tommy flew high up in the sky into the storm clouds. Suddenly he was up there, gliding in the wind like a predatory hawk, and he was unafraid. Below on Earth, he saw the little wood where they were camped slip away with the dark and nature. Night animals and coyotes howled and pointed their muzzles at his passing.

He flew over the mountains. Saw snow for the first time in his life. Saw people's houses, their farms, their stables. Saw their pretentious cities, but from up there they were nothing. He entered a dark forest where there was only silence.

He found the oak tree, which was ancient and immense. Its roots held down the world. Tommy the Hawk glided to his feet under the green canopy of its branches, so thick and wide he could no longer see the sky.

He stayed there feeling his heart beating, and imagined that Chief Tecumseh had now become one with the trunk, the bark, the branches, the leaves and the acorns; and from there he continued to watch over the *Shawnee's* lands.

All the birds of passage would alight on his gnarled arms and every forest animal would come at least once to render him homage.

The old man had fallen asleep in front of the fire.

In the morning, when Tommy woke up, the embers were cold and what remained of the tribe had resumed their journey.

'Little Black Wolf, eh?' said Peg Leg Joe. 'Perhaps Little Polecat's better.'

After a day and a half of walking, they finally caught sight of the Station the Guide had promised them, where they would find comfort and shelter.

They were all exhausted.

In the first uncertain light of dawn a beautiful farmhouse appeared, one of the best they had ever seen. It was large, well cared for, clean, with a newly repainted porch and stable, a hay barn, a well and flowered curtains at the windows. They instinctively quickened their step.

The fields all around were abundant and well-tended with corn, barley and oats. A thread of smoke came from the chimney, and for certain a good breakfast was laid out on the table for them. They imagined milk and cream, and bread just out of the over and *bacon* . . . Reeling with exhaustion, everyone had his dream.

They ran the last few yards.

Peg Leg Joe jumped up the four steps of the veranda and knocked confidently.

The door opened and a white man appeared, a rifle gripped in his hand.

Fourteen

They stopped, paralysed.

It was a trap.

Someone had blabbed.

Someone had been dazzled by those hundred dollars in gold – worth a herd – and had sold out.

Tommy felt his legs grow as heavy as lead and his stomach contract painfully, then he felt an irresistible urge to escape.

'Run! Run! Run Tommy, don't get caught!' But he could never run faster than a gunshot. And where to? He neither had the strength, nor the will.

How many weeks had they been on the road?

Tommy thought about it.

He looked at Papa and Mamma and saw the same disbelieving bewilderment on their faces.

The white man at the door was big and fat, his face sunburned and his flaming hair a shade of incredible red. He wore enormous working man's boots and faded blue overalls straining over his stomach.

He looked at the sky clearing to the east.

'Today should be a good day for shooting starlings,' he said leaning his rifle carefully against the veranda railing.

'Hello Kurtz,' said Peg Leg Joe.

'Come in,' said the white man.

Peg Leg Joe signalled, 'Come in! Come in!'

No one moved.

'Come in, I'm telling you.'

They went in slowly, one at a time, dragging their feet in front of the door.

They found themselves in a big kitchen laid with wooden floorboards, an enormous stove and a row of shining copper saucepans hung on the walls and on a shelf. There were plates, bowls, a funnel – Tommy recognised it – and a box with a little door and on the top, a handle, which he didn't know, but even from a distance smelled of coffee. There was a laden table.

As Tommy looked at it, his eyes widened. He felt his stomach contract again, not out of fear this time, but hunger.

There had never been all those things in their kitchen at home.

His Mamma alongside him was very embarrassed. Sammy and his wife didn't know where to look and what to do with their hands.

No Negro ever entered a white man's house, at least, not unless he was a servant. What's more, they were dirty and smelly and in rags, and there was not a speck of dust in this kitchen.

Standing beside the table were a white woman, two white boys, a white girl, and a brown dog.

The dog wagged his tail and came up to Tommy, sniffed him and began nibbling at a big toe sticking out of a broken shoe.

Tommy didn't know how to behave with white dogs.

True, but this one was brown.

'Sit down, brothers,' said the white man who was clearly the head of the family.

Peg Leg Joe was as calm and relaxed as if he was in his own home, and repeated their host's invitation to sit down. He ceremoniously greeted the mistress of the house and caressed the children before sitting at the table as instructed.

The white man at the head of the table said a prayer the same as the one they said at home and they all answered, 'Amen.'

Then they all ate with gusto.

The owners of the house asked them nothing, neither who they were, nor where they came from. Only the white woman asked Mamma how the journey had been up till then.

'Oh,' replied Mamma, who didn't know what to say.

'You must be exhausted.'

'Oh, yes, we are.'

'I've prepared some beds in the hay barn,' said the woman. 'The straw is fresh and soft.'

'Thank you,' said Mamma.

Then they chatted about this and that as you do over breakfast.

Peg Leg Joe asked Kurtz about the weather and the harvest. He replied that the next day he would have to do some weeding.

'I'll give you a hand,' offered Papa.

'Maybe it's better that you rest,' replied the red-haired giant.

'After all these weeks of running away, a bit of work would be a pleasure,' said Papa.

There, he had said it: running away. Nothing happened.

It was just like home.

The two white boys waited a good while before kicking Tommy under the table, as he'd expected they would. Then one of them pinched Daisy Mae who cried.

The two mammas – one white and one black – slapped everyone all round without distinguishing between race or colour and peace was restored.

And so it was, that after the meal all the girls were sent to wash up the plates and saucepans and all of them, without distinction of race or colour, protested that it wasn't fair and why did they always have to do it.

The white woman then escorted them to the hay barn where she had prepared beds of the softest straw. Just before falling asleep with a full stomach, Tommy saw his mother talking non-stop with the white lady, doubtless about women's things. White people seemed just like them. How incredible!

'The Kurtz family are Quakers. Their religion is against slavery,' explained Peg Leg Joe. 'There are lots of Stations where they are. We'll find others on our way.'

'So there are good white people?' asked Tommy.

Peg Leg Joe was carving a piece of soft wood with a knife to pass the time. He wasn't intending to carve anything in particular. They had been at the Kurtz family home for two days with the order not to show themselves out in the open, unless after sunset, and to stay indoors in the stable. At last, they could rest, laze around, do nothing.

In the evening they would go out onto the threshing floor to enjoy the fresh air and the gentle landscape of hills and fields of rye and oats while waiting for Mrs Kurtz to call them for the supper which she had prepared with Mamma.

'There are good white people like there are bad Negroes, and I imagine it's like that everywhere for everyone. In the North almost all the white people are for the abolition of slavery, and it will happen, sooner or later, I betcha.'

'Do you believe that one day there will be no slaves anymore?' asked Tommy.

'It will happen, but it will take time.'

'But they're all mean to the Indians.'

'Oh, the Indians. There will be none of them left. The ones who are left . . . well, I don't know much about what a reservation is. A sort of pen I think. They can't put people in a pen, like animals,' said Peg Leg Joe.

'It's not right!'

'No, it's not right.'

'I have to tell you something.'

'You're more irritating than a horsefly!'

Tommy blurted out what had been tormenting him for days all in one breath; sentences overlapped and tripped over his tongue.

Peg Leg Joe listened attentively, then spoke, 'Good. Talk to your father about it.' And he returned to carving his piece of wood.

Tommy had confided his most important secret in him; had let him know of a most important decision, but what did Peg Leg Joe do? Nothing. He had hoped that Peg Leg Joe would look at him differently, that he would say he was proud of him, and that they would shake on it like men do.

'There's no sense in talking to my father, he wouldn't understand,' the boy grumbled. 'Mamma would die of fright if I said things like that to her. You know how they are. Papa's not brave like you. He wouldn't get it. He wants me to become a farmhand like him when I grow up and can't imagine anything else.'

Peg Leg Joe's index finger reared up threateningly in front of Tommy's nose. It was as big as a banana.

'Just you listen to me, young man. One more word and I'll take your pants down and belt you. For sure. It's what you need.'

Peg Leg Joe's hands were as big as hams, or two shovels. Tommy fell silent as he tried to imagine the effect they would have on his backside. What had he done wrong?

'And now listen, you presumptuous, ignorant little boy. Your father accepted a life of hardship and humiliation for you and your sisters. For the love of you, he bowed his head and said, "Yes sir, no sir." He acted stupid, like a clever Negro has to with white people. He laughed when white men made a fool of him, as a clever, obedient Negro must do. He learned to stay silent, never to say one word. He put a muzzle on his pride. What's the sense in rebelling against the whites for them to strip the flesh off your back with whippings? Would it have helped you or your sisters? When I came to your village and played *Steal Away*, only he and Sammy understood. Only they came to me during the night. Only they found the courage to run away. Do you know why? Because Sammy loves his wife. Because your father loves you and doesn't want you to live as slaves. That's your father.

Sure, he's a farmhand, and knows nothing about the world. Sure, he has little imagination and can't see a life for you and your sisters much different than having a bit of land and living on it. But he dreams of a better life. And a free one. And has the courage to achieve it. Dammit.'

Peg Leg Joe left.

Tommy felt his face burn and his ears ring. It was the first time his friend had walked out on him. He would almost have preferred a good spanking.

He woke at dusk, after a long refreshing sleep. The setting sun had set the horizon on fire along with the crowns of the trees and the stubble-covered maize fields. The air was pure and peaceful.

Tommy looked for his father and found him. Sitting alongside each other under the big elm tree dominating the threshing floor, they remained silent for a while. Each chewed on a grass stalk lost in reverie, and followed the black lines of crows flying across the sky. It felt harmonious.

Two days before, thanks to the Quakers' support network, packages of clean clothes, shirts, work overalls and heavy jackets for the approaching winter had started to arrive on the quiet. And shoes! Shoes at last!

Mamma had laboured at the zinc tub which took up almost the entire little room at the back of the farmhouse. She scrubbed him so furiously, Tommy thought she would skin him. It was worth it. They were well-fed and clean at last; dressed in new clothes.

In the peace of the evening, Papa chewed on his leaf and watched Tommy.

His son had grown during the past weeks, regardless of their trials, as children always do. He was now taller and stronger, and had matured.

He had become great friends with Peg Leg Joe, and he was glad of that. Joe was someone who had much to teach a curious boy. And Tommy was definitely curious.

He was glad of the boy's friendship with Peg Leg Joe as the man had much to teach a curious boy who had always been curious, ever since he was little.

He was inquisitive, always getting into trouble. Papa smiled at the memory.

'I want to learn to read,' said Tommy suddenly with his back turned and his eyes fixed on some vague point on the horizon.

'Why?' asked Papa.

'To understand things,' said Tommy.

Papa hesitated, surprised. He remained silent.

The crows were flocking together on the highest branches of the elm tree and making a tremendous din. It was the best time of the day.

His son, the son of a slave, learning to read! Papa had never dreamed of such a thing. Up until a while ago it would have seemed to him not only impossible, but a bit of a sacrilege. Unnatural in fact.

A slave, reading!

So much had changed since he had slipped out of the cabin that night, trembling from fear and confusion, to talk to the stranger with the wooden leg and ask him what he had meant by the song he'd sung?

The man had explained. In turn, Papa had explained it to Mamma and they had not slept a wink, but had kept looking into each other's eyes and hugging each other to give themselves courage.

The anguish and fear of making a mistake was great.

They had changed their minds a thousand times.

So much had changed in those weeks since their flight, and there'd be more changes if they got to Canaan or Canada, or whatever the place was called; that land where all men were free and equal.

'And then,' continued Tommy, 'I want to learn to play the banjo and sing the songs that Peg Leg Joe sings.'

'Why?' asked Papa.

Tommy's reply took a long time coming, 'I want to become a Guide . . . and free all the slaves.'

Papa looked at his boy as he had never looked at him before.

Despite Tommy's back being turned, Papa did not see a child, but the strong and decisive man that his son would become. And he saw a free man.

First his heart contracted in fear, then it widened like a smile. It contracted once more, because he understood that his son was asking him if he might fly far away from him and that from now on he would be more Peg Leg Joe's than his. And he wanted his father's blessing.

Papa thought about the hardship and the dangers. The long nights and the ambushes. You can lose a son in so many other ways, life and destiny sometimes know how to be cruel and as hard as a flint. He knew that very well.

He thought fast about what he could do to dissuade him from this plan.

Then he thought he didn't want to talk him out of it, and his heart melted.

Then he stopped thinking about it. And forgot it.

He didn't know what to say, and the crows were making such a racket, his words would have been drowned out anyway.

He squeezed his son's fragile shoulders very hard. It seemed impossible that they could grow stronger.

The boy stayed with his back turned.

'Damn!' said Papa, almost shouting to cover up his swearing. 'Now we've got to go tell Mamma. She'll be very angry.'

'You tell her,' said Tommy.

'No way! It's up to you.'

'No way . . . Damn,' said Tommy. 'She'll be angry at both of us.'

'You may be right,' said Papa.

They plucked up their courage and went together towards the kitchen.

Fifteen

. . . Where the great big river
meet the little river
Follow the Drinking Gourd
for the Old Man is waiting for
to carry you to freedom
if you follow the Drinking Gourd . . .

Following the Drinking Gourd night after night, they had arrived at the enormous river which they sang about in the last verse of the song.

Ohio River was huge. It crossed the territory also called Ohio, just as the Tennessee had crossed Tennessee. These were two states of the United States of America: a continent so enormous that when the sun was rising in one part, it was setting in another. But Tommy wasn't swallowing that, because there's only one sun, right? Everybody knows that.

Sometimes he thought Peg Leg Joe was making fun of him.

But the Old Man leading them to freedom had to be respected.

Every day now, Peg Leg Joe woke him up at least an hour before they set off, or when the sun was setting (if they had to travel by night), or at its first rays (if it was safe to travel by day). In all cases, Tommy was fast asleep.

He would mumble, grumble, roll up in his blanket and pull it over his head saying, 'Not today.' Or he'd say, 'I've got a terrible tummy ache.'

'You've got the lightning point for that,' replied Peg Leg Joe.

'It's not a lightning point! It's an arrowhead. You thought I didn't know? You tricked me!'

'It's not true!'

Then he got up and washed his face with cold water.

Luckily, on some days, there was no water, but that didn't happen often.

He would eat and, dragging his feet, followed Peg Leg Joe; enviously looking at the others sleeping blissfully, especially those two lazybones sisters of his.

'Why do they sleep late and not me?'

'Because they don't want to learn to read, and you do.'

'I don't either.'

'Walk,' said Peg Leg Joe who showed no mercy.

He led the boy to a quiet spot, had him sit down on the ground beside him, patted down a bit of earth with his big hand so as to make a smooth surface to use like a blackboard, and held a sharpened stick to use as a pen. The lesson would then begin.

Peg Leg Joe drew the letters of the alphabet on the ground, then wiped them off with a swipe, and it was Tommy's turn to hold the stick.

'From the beginning. Again.'

Tommy grumbled, but he learned everything in a flash, even though he had a great deal to do, because he was also learning how to play the banjo.

Besides the alphabet, there were the verses of Peg Leg Joe's songs to learn by heart, and Peg Leg Joe knew so many. Consequently Tommy's fingertips would bleed from practising so much on steel strings.

He tried especially hard to play the Drinking Gourd song well, because every Guide knew it – there wasn't one who didn't – and later he would learn *Steal Away* and after that . . .

'Do you think one day I'll know Harriet's song?' he asked anxiously.

'If you play like that she'll run away!'

There was another song he was learning which he liked a lot:

Oh freedom, oh freedom,
oh freedom over me
and before I'll be a slave
I'll be buried in my grave
and go home to my Lord
and be free.

Every now and again when he was in the mood, and they were in a place where it was safe to play a banjo, Peg Leg Joe would pluck the strings and play sad, strange songs that were different from the usual ones . . . Some didn't even sound like songs, but were more like laments, or cries for help. One very long one dragged on and on . . .

Woh hoo-oo, woh hoo!
Woh hoo-oo, woh hoo!

It was a heart-rending cry which made you shiver.

'What does it mean?' they would all ask.

'It means: *Woh hoo-oo . . .*'

Others consisted of a few words repeated endlessly and did not say much:

Bring me a little water, Sylvie,
Bring me a little water now . . .

Hearing it made you sad and brought a lump to your throat as Tommy said. After a bit someone would say, 'Joe, play us something cheerful.'

'This is Negro music, my friend,' he would reply. 'It's a music of work, sweat and exhaustion. What reason does a Negro have to be cheerful? Do you know where these songs are born? From the rear end of a mule, excuse my language. Because if you're a stinking slave and you walk behind everyone in a convoy attached to the tail of the last mule . . . what music would you compose to pass the time, eh? What you're feeling, you invent.'

Tommy didn't have a minute's peace.

Did anyone tell him well done?

Peg Leg Joe went around saying that Tommy was the shabbiest banjo player he'd ever known – and he'd known lots. The boy was as out of tune as a cow before milking – and he'd known plenty of cows too, you'd better believe it!

Tommy got very very angry. He may have been out of tune, but he was a champion at the alphabet. He'd learned a lot.

Day after day, a bit at a time, Peg Leg Joe began placing one letter after the other. 'What's that?'

'. . . f . .' said Tommy

'What's that?'

'. . . r . .'

'And that?'

'. . . e . .'

'Read.'

'f . . . r . . . e . . . e,' spelled out Tommy.

'Go on.'

'. . . d . . . o . . . m . . . Freedom!'

'*Freedom*,' repeated Peg Leg Joe. 'Liberty. Like the name of the song you're learning. This is your first word. Read it to your father and mother as soon as they wake up.'

Of course they had no book.

But Peg Leg Joe fished something out of the depths of his travelling bag, and held it out to Tommy like a reliquary. It was a sheet of paper folded in four, yellowed with age and damp.

'At the next Station the Quakers will probably be happy to get you a Bible. You'll have enough to read for your whole life. Meanwhile, use this to practise,' he said. 'It's something that concerns all of us.'

Tommy unfolded the old sheet being careful not to tear it, as it was so thin and worn. It was a printed poster, the kind you sometimes see stuck on a wall.

He had seen them for example when he had gone with Papa to the emporium to fetch the goods ordered by Captain Archer. There were always posters there. He couldn't understand what they said, and even Papa couldn't explain what they meant. But some had pretty coloured pictures.

The one he was holding now didn't have any pictures. A jumble of letters and signs covered the whole page. He lost heart.

'One letter at a time,' suggested Peg Leg Joe. 'You have plenty of time. I need to wake the others and break camp. You stay here and work at it.'

Tommy looked at the sheet, pulled at his nose, scratched his head. He didn't understand a thing. Reading was too difficult.

Then two letters came together mysteriously, and a third and a fourth and a fifth. Tommy couldn't believe his eyes, they came together by themselves, he didn't have to do it at all. Was that reading?

They were BIG letters at the top of the poster. Perhaps that was why it was easier to read them.

He spelled out the word slowly to himself, 'S.'

S . . . L . . . A . . . V . . . E . . . S . . . That was what was written. He was amazed: those black marks on that piece of paper had become something real. The world was full of black letters which were waiting to be discovered. And he knew how to do it! So that was reading?

Then, almost without realising it, he read the two words, written smaller, which were before the big word, '**Sale of** . . .' he said aloud, '**SALE OF SLAVES**.'

His heart beat very fast. He was unlocking a secret, and would find out something that the others – his father, mother, sisters – could never know. But he would! Confusedly, he understood that doing this made him strong.

Slaves knew nothing, and had no way to know anything: neither when they were born, nor in which county they lived, or what year it was and what lay beyond the hedges and fences marking out their master's property. They were like oxen which did not know what was outside their stable and were content to chew their grass. That way they remained slaves forever.

'Tommy,' called his mother. 'Come and eat.'

The others had got up and were massaging their backs, sore from the hard ground. They were having a good stretch, and preparing their bundles to go on the march again.

As he did every morning, Peg Leg Joe would complain about how much he wanted to have a coffee. It was a strange habit he'd picked up when he lived in a town, none of them had ever drunk coffee until now.

'A white man's habit,' Papa would say when he wanted to tease him.

Tommy folded the sheet carefully and put it safely between his skin and his shirt: **SALE OF SLAVES**. He couldn't get it out of his head.

From that day on, Tommy took advantage of every stop, of every moment's pause to read the poster. He sat far away from the others, slipped his hand inside his shirt, unfolded the piece of paper and began spelling it out, wrinkling his forehead from the effort, and moving his lips little by little as he spelled out the letters.

It took him many days because the text was long. Some passages made no sense so he asked Peg Leg Joe. He finally managed to decipher almost everything.

Naturally, Tommy knew all about being a black slave, the son of black slaves. He knew about slavery from personal experience: that a slave is his master's property, who can do what he wants with him. He knew that he could be sold and transferred to another farm a long way from his parents. These things happened all the time. There were men who were left on their own because their wife had been sold. There were parents whose children had been snatched from them. He knew it all. But seeing it written on a piece of paper was different. It was much worse.

The poster had been printed by some gentlemen called *Hewlett & Bright*. They were proud to be, 'an old and respected firm specialising in the buying and selling of slaves of proven quality. Never a complaint from our esteemed clients.'

It announced a special sale on Sunday 16 May at noon, on the corner of St Louis Street, in a city called New Orleans.

The merchandise for sale was listed:

Sarah, aged 45, an excellent cook and housekeeper.

Sarah's son Dennis, aged 24, strong and healthy, an honest boy with no bad habits, trustworthy.

Dandridge, aged 26, excellent for fieldwork, offered alongside his wife Nancy who had no particular virtues listed, except the fact that she was very attractive.

Mary-Ann, their daughter, Creole, age 7.

Emma, age 10, or perhaps 11 or 12, an orphan.

Would someone want to buy an orphan? She was cheap.

There was a guarantee that none of them had any infectious diseases.

Tommy read and re-read those names.

He tried to picture their faces and their voices; conjure up what Mary-Ann, age 7, was thinking at night after she finished sweeping the kitchen; lifting a bucket of dirty water weighing more than her and going to empty it outside in the pigsty, before finally getting to her bed under the stairs.

He tried to picture Emma, who was his age, tried to imagine her all alone, standing on a makeshift stage, on a street corner in that unknown city called New Orleans, with everyone looking at her, dying of shame and longing to hide . . . waiting for an unknown man who would come up to her, size her up to see what she was worth, put his hands in her mouth to examine her teeth. Having taken out his wallet and paid, he would take her away who knows where, to do who knows what.

It was unimaginable, he could not conceive such a thing. Just a void.

Sixteen

'We have to cross it,' said Peg Leg Joe. 'There's no other way.'

They were high up on a grass-covered hill overlooking a city which spread out before them in the valley below. None of them had ever seen a city, except the Guide. It seemed to take up the whole valley, as far as the eye could see.

There were rows and rows of houses unlike the farms they were used to, all piled one on top of the other, with streets running between them. Even from up there, the runaways could imagine swarms of people, horses and cars thronging the place.

On one side the city was lapped by the waters of the river whose course they had been following for weeks. On the other, there was an intricate network of railway tracks, with the station and its platform roof. A water tank and row upon row of corrals were set to one side, where the herds were massed, arriving from the West after weeks of being herded across mountains and plains, to wait to be loaded onto wagons and sent to market in the big cities on the east coast.

They had heard about the railway, but it was distant and unreal. Now they could see it for themselves. A sharp, prolonged whistle reached them from the valley bottom, muffled by distance. It was repeated several times, and they saw a plume of black smoke rise up from the plain and grow bigger. A few minutes later the locomotive was in the station pulling its convoy behind it. Even from up there, it was impressive and powerful, a mass of iron and unstoppable steam. It was frightening.

Hundreds of people streamed out of the coaches. Even up there, they could hear the shouts of the porters and see black servants lifting suitcases into the carriages and *calèches*, and then swarm towards the centre of town.

'It's the cattle fair,' explained Peg Leg Joe, 'one of the biggest and most important. It goes on a whole week. Breeders and buyers come from every state. And tomorrow there's the rodeo. Yes siree! There are people who wear out their behinds in the saddle for a whole week, so they don't miss it.'

'The rodeo?' asked Tommy.

'Yeahhh! Wild horses to break in. Calves to lasso and tie up before you can count to ten. Bulls to ride.'

'Bulls . . . ?'

'A bit of fun. Someone always goes home with broken bones, you betcha. A big party. Chaos. Night and day. Rivers of whisky. It's better that way. In the confusion no one will take any notice of us.'

Papa and Mamma and Sammy and everyone were breathless with fear. The city was unfamiliar and hostile. Full of unknown, mysterious things. Even the air seemed thick and dark. Along the river, tall scorched brick chimneys rose up against the sky, erupting fire and smoke.

They looked at one another to give themselves courage.

'Factories,' explained Peg Leg Joe.

None of them had even seen a proper village before.

Outside Captain Archer's plantation, what they thought was a village – a place called Ludon – was really a handful of cabins with an emporium, a blacksmith, a barbershop with a taproom attached. It was a settlement at the crossroads of various plantations.

The Negro servants went there on errands, and the white overseers to drain a bottle in peace. A stranger rarely passed by, and if such a thing did happen, it was because he had lost his way.

During those months of journeying they had kept far away from everyone to avoid being detected, living in rivers, forests, the undergrowth, ravines and caves whenever necessary. At best, some farm, or cabin provided for them, thanks to the grapevine telegraph.

The idea of now entering the city terrified them. Besides, it was a city full of white people.

'It will be like you say, Joe,' said Papa. "But they'll find us straightaway and we'll be done for. They'll realise that . . . we're not . . .' He stammered as he tried to find the right words.

The others nodded in agreement.

'There's no way round it,' explained Peg Leg Joe. 'The bridge over the river is on the other side. To get there we have to cross the city. That bridge will take us directly to Illinois.'

'Do you mean,' asked Papa hesitatingly, 'that we're about to reach Canada?'

Peg Leg Joe felt the weight of seven pairs of eyes waiting for his reply.

They were exhausted, having walked up the Ohio River and made detour after detour, losing time, so as to avoid the urban centres which had become more frequent. The air had grown piercingly cold, making them shiver in their flimsy clothes, until the grapevine telegraph had provided a bundle of shawls, big woollen sweaters and heavy shoes of the kind that made it difficult to lift your feet.

They had continued to head north following the Drinking Gourd and stopping at Stations where anonymous black and white people risked their lives to protect and help them reach freedom.

And now, finally, Peg Leg Joe was saying that they were about to reach Canada – wasn't he?

'No,' he said, 'Canada is still far away. But Illinois is on the other side of the river where slavery is illegal. That doesn't mean that we can go easy, we must still be cautious because they could catch us and send us back. It'd be difficult, but it has been known to happen. At least we've almost made it. We're not yet in Canaan but we're about to leave Egypt!'

Everyone hugged one another and whooped three cheers for the Guide.

'Listen carefully,' said Peg Leg Joe. 'To get to Illinois, means crossing that city. And the bridge. It's dangerous. The bridge is watched by an armed guard, night and day. They know runaway slaves pass there. But there's no other way so we have to do it.' He looked into their eyes, one by one.

'If we've got as far as here,' said Papa, 'we'll get beyond that bridge. It would be a cruel joke to stop just one step away from freedom.'

'Right,' said Peg Leg Joe. 'Now here's what we do . . .'

Main Street was like a river in full flood, threatening to sweep them away at any moment.

Smelly cowboys with wide leather trousers and beards that could prick you just by looking at them; dandies in waistcoats and silk neckties; barefoot farmhands who had come to town for the rodeo, glancing around almost as lost as Tommy; distinguished, well-dressed gentlemen who kept to the wooden sidewalks at the sides of the streets so as not to dirty their shoes, who looked at the rabble contemptuously; white men; black men; yellow men with narrowed oval eyes and a plait bouncing about their shoulders; an Indian in a bowler hat who clutched his pipe and silently cut through the crowd with an air of indifference.

Men of every kind, dressed in the strangest fashions, shouted, swore, laughed, bumped and shoved one another in the middle of the dusty road where horses, wagons, and *calèches* went by heedless, threatening to trample anyone who got in their way, too slow to move aside.

'Make way! Make way!' yelled the drivers.

Tommy held on tightly to his father's hand, hoping not to be run over or swept away. He walked head down, fast, but he couldn't resist taking the occasional peek.

The city was full of strange and marvellous things . . . Shops. Huge, gaudy painted wooden signs. Emporium. Drug Store. Barber Shop. *Guns.* And there was the blacksmith, the stables for the horses.

There was the saloon with swing doors which clacked each time someone went in or out, and they did that continuously, because the rodeo made everyone tremendously thirsty.

There were banners decorated with big rosettes strung from one side of the street to the other. Tommy didn't have time to decipher what was written on them, but he assumed they announced the cattle fair, the rodeo, and other events.

Even though he was petrified and convinced that the flood of people could sweep him away to be lost forever, he thought he would like to stay in the city even if for only one day, to wander around, look at everything, and be at the rodeo.

Wild horses. Bulls to ride.

He stumbled and almost toppled over, so caught hold of Papa's hand again.

Peg Leg Joe had divided them into little groups to avoid being noticed. 'The place will be full of Negroes. Slaves following masters, servants going about on errands, loafers who never miss an opportunity to wander about and enjoy the festival. They'll be coming from all the plantations round about, you can be sure of that. Ahhhh, when there's a rodeo there's partying, I'm telling you. No one will notice us. But we must split up, we can't all be seen together. And we'll leave these behind,' he added, pointing to the threadbare bags and bundles which they had carried all those months. 'They would betray us for what we are – fugitives. We'll take the bare minimum.'

'Oh, our things . . .' moaned Mamma.

'Beyond the bridge,' said the Guide, 'there's a Station. They're waiting for us. They've known about our arrival for days. They'll find us everything we need for the last part of our journey. If someone gets lost, or something happens . . . Watch out! Nothing will happen, but if it does . . . Stay where you are. I'll come and get you. Off we go!'

'Amen!' they chorused.

'*Yeahhhhh!*'

Peg Leg Joe went on ahead, his banjo slung over his back, to show the way. He was so tall that it was enough to look up and see his head sticking up above the crowd. Tommy followed twenty paces behind with Papa, who was carrying an old rusty hoe he'd picked up in a field over his shoulder, so as to look like a farmhand come to the city for his master. Mamma was further back with the girls. She balanced on her head a basket with the few things they had taken with them, looking just like a *Mammy* sent by her mistress to buy things at the emporium: a bottle of *eau de cologne*, some cosmetics . . . Sammy and his wife, who didn't need a disguise, followed. They rolled their eyes in surprise at everything, frightened and confused, so no one would question whether they were two stupid Negro bumpkins from some nearby farm who had slipped through the back door to come and see the festivities. Their master would make them pay if he discovered their deception when they went back.

The runaways advanced slowly, being bumped and shoved. Main Street seemed to go on forever. Peg Leg Joe turned round every now and again with a careless air, to check they were following him.

They had waited until sunset to move so that they would reach the bridge when it was still light. The sun was sinking behind the wooden houses and the railway water tank, and the shadows lengthened on the red dust of the road.

Had they started to cross the city under cover of night, the darkness would have protected them and nothing would have happened. But that would have meant running the risk of losing sight of one another, and losing their bearings. They could have stayed together as a group and helped one another. But that was too risky, they would have been too noticeable.

Perhaps it was just fate.

Who knows why things happen?

They happen, and that's that.

Sammy and Sarah walked close together, bewildered, sweating with fear, jostled by the crowd. They were afraid to lose sight of the others and Peg Leg Joe, of getting confused, or going the wrong way, of being run over by a cart, of arousing the curiosity of one of the drunks, 'Hey *nigger* who d'you think you are? I asked you a question. And who might that be, your little wife? Hey blackface, I'm talking to you . . .'

They didn't look where they were putting their feet, which is how they bumped into a man standing stock still in the middle of Main Street. He was big and fat, and was planted in the middle of the crowd, cutting it in two like a pillar dividing a river. His Mexican boots had twinkling spurs. His hat was brand new, and he had a lasso coiled around his shoulder. He was probably in the city for the rodeo, or perhaps he was a horse-breeder looking for mustangs for his ranch.

The man turned around. His sunburned face had been made even redder by the many glasses of alcohol he had drunk. He was very angry.

'Hey, Negro!' he shouted. 'You, Negro! How dare you, Negro!?'

His voice was big and rough. So much so that Peg Leg Joe heard it above the din of the crowd, as did Papa who recognised it, and shuddered. The two men turned round at the same time.

'I'm talking to you, stinking Negro. Who are you? Who's your master?'

They knew that voice very well. And that sunburned face too. It was Jim Kniff in his best boots.

Seventeen

J im Kniff had worn his behind to the bone riding day after day, in sun and rain, so as not to miss his appointment with the great rodeo and the most important Horse Fair of the year. He would return driving in front of him a dozen wild mustangs for Captain Archer's stock farm and a bay stallion for his personal use – if he could find the right one.

Real horses, like real men, are always the most difficult to find. In truth, they're all nags.

As soon as he had reached the city, he shaved, washed and perfumed himself so he was spick and span. He was dressed in his best, had made a tour of the saloons, and amply slaked his thirst to clear his throat of the journey's dust. He had lost twenty dollars at poker, and watched two fights. The festivities had just begun and it was already looking as if they would be good ones.

Now, a little bit tipsy, he had stopped in the centre of Main Street, heedless of the crowd surrounding him and the carters shouting wildly as they advanced, to decide whether he would allow himself another little glass before going to supper at a place where they knew him and where he'd never been disappointed. They grilled wonderfully thick steaks.

Then that Negro had bumped into him. He'd never put up with something like that. Give a Negro an inch and he'll take a mile.

The culprit had begun to snivel an apology, 'Sorry, Master, sorry.'

They always do that, Negroes are totally false. Even the girl who was with him, his wife or whatever, was begging, hands clasped. That girl . . . To Jim Kniff, slaves were all alike. Just black faces. Impossible to tell them apart, he couldn't do it.

He could recognise a horse by the way it neighed. And could single out a cow in the herd by a fold of an ear. Not Negroes, though. All the same, they were animals.

But Sarah was very beautiful. He recognised her immediately.

She had long smooth hair, not the usual curly fuzz, and amber skin. She knew how to move gracefully.

Although she was a Negress, Jim Kniff had looked at her more than once as she walked through the furrows in the cotton fields bringing water to the pickers, or when she was ordered to Captain Archer's house for some service or other.

Jim Kniff had the honour of lunching at the Captain's table once a week and had seen and admired her countless times.

'Fugitives! They're fugitives!' he yelled.

A wall of backs blocked Tommy's view, so he couldn't see what was happening. One lot of people had stopped to enjoy the spectacle, while others turned around, colliding with those who had continued on their way.

He heard Jim Kniff's voice clearly, and Sammy's pleading.

It was over.

Their flight had ended one step from safety.

Jim Kniff had finally found them.

Tommy felt Papa tremble and squeeze his hand more tightly as he stopped. The boy realised his father wanted to go and help Sammy.

'Keep walking,' said a voice, loud and clear.

Mamma was looking around in dismay, embracing the girls as if to protect them with her arms as wings. She also heard the message.

'Keep walking . . .'

Jim Kniff had seized Sammy by the worn collar of his shirt. 'The others must be here too!'

Tommy could barely manage a single step, his legs were trembling so much.

'Keep walking and don't turn around.'

One, two, three steps . . . 'They'll catch us,' whispered the boy. It was impossible, they'd be recognised.

Tommy felt Jim Kniff's look burning like fire through the crowd. The overseer held Sammy by the neck and spurred on other white men to track down the runaways.

Tommy felt hundreds of eyes piercing his back. His hand was so sweaty it was difficult to hold on to Papa's hand.

'There are more of them!' shouted Jim Kniff.

'They'll catch us...'

The crowd rippled.

Any minute, a drunken farmhand could point them out . . . 'There they are! There they are!' . . . 'Runaway slaves!' . . . 'A hundred dollars in gold!'

He tried to see his mother, and couldn't. Perhaps they'd already caught her.

'Don't turn around!' said Peg Leg Joe, slowly cleaving his way through the crowd at the side, edging his way a little at a time towards a side street. The runaways followed.

'To the sheriff's office!' shouted Jim Kniff.

How far to go . . . thirty steps . . . twenty steps?

The side street was an alley of trodden earth wedged in amongst wooden houses. It was deserted. They went down it and slid to the ground in the shade, trying to get their breath back and calm their beating hearts. The river of people continued to flow past just a few metres away.

Even Peg Leg Joe's face looked ashen.

For several minutes no one spoke.

No one had noticed them! Jim Kniff's big sun blotched face didn't loom into the entrance to the alley.

'It'll be dark in a little while,' said Peg Leg Joe. 'And then I'll go and get them.'

'We'll go,' said Papa. 'How did that Harriet put it? We don't leave anyone behind. Isn't that right?'

'I'm coming too!' offered Tommy.

'No way,' said Papa. 'You stay with your mother and sisters, and no buts. Obey me!'

Tommy had rarely seen his father so determined.

'You must get to the river and wait for us there,' said Peg Leg Joe. 'You will have to lead the children, ma'am,' he added, turning to Mamma, 'if you're up to it?'

Mamma calmed her trembling hands and took a deep breath, 'Tell me what I have to do, Joe.'

'Follow Main Street, straight on, without turning off. Don't look in anyone's face. Don't stop. You'll get to the river, you can't go wrong. Find a hiding place and wait for us there. We'll find you.'

'Sure,' said Mamma in an uncertain voice.

Papa hugged her, 'You can do it.'

'If that Harriet crossed America six times, I'll manage to get to the river, won't I?' she said.

They waited. The sun had set a little while ago. The alley was a black pool of darkness. The crowd on Main Street had thinned out.

'Let's go,' said the Guide.

Papa hugged everyone.

'If we don't see you . . .' said Mamma voicing everyone's thoughts.

'We'll be there, don't you worry,' said Papa.

'We'll be there with Sammy and Sarah,' said Peg Leg Joe.

Mamma took the children, paused to check the coast was clear and turned into the main street. Tommy turned around for a last glimpse of his father and the Guide. It was dark and he was still in turmoil, but as the clouds parted, he was certain that in the light of the sickle moon, he saw Peg Leg Joe take a metal object out of his bag and slip it into the belt of his trousers.

It took a moment. Then the sickle moon immediately disappeared.

Tommy followed his mother, holding the smaller of his sisters by the hand. He'd seen it clearly, he was sure of it. A shiny six shooter like the one Harriet Tubman carried under her skirt.

Tommy prayed that his father and Peg Leg Joe wouldn't have to use it.

Eighteen

Jim Kniff had dragged Sammy and Sarah to the sheriff's office at the bottom of Main Street. He had locked the runaways in the cell while Old Johnson held open the door.

'Fugitives, eh?' was all he said, stroking his tobacco-stained moustache. Old Johnson was very likely in his last term of office as sheriff. He was too old by several years and had a bad back. The city was growing fast and to keep it in line required someone younger and more resourceful than he was nowadays. The powers that be might even send a federal sheriff as a replacement.

He had a little ranch out towards the mountains, a quiet place that suited him, where he would retire. He knew Jim Kniff and realised it was pointless asking too many questions.

Jim Kniff had gone off to enjoy his steak, three fingers thick, but he had no peace of mind. There was something gnawing at him. He'd caught two of them, granted. But the others had escaped. They had managed to get lost in the crowd and had probably already left the city by now. He had neither men nor means to organise a search.

Old Johnson wouldn't have given them to him anyway, that much he knew. The old sheriff didn't want trouble. He would keep the two captives in jail and send them back to Captain Archer's plantation. He wouldn't ask what the future held in store for them.

Jim Kniff was of the opinion that what happened to runaways when they were caught should serve as an example to others. That way it'd deter them from trying to pull off the same stunt. A harsh lesson needed to be taught, no point being subtle. But he couldn't expect anything like that from Johnson.

Jim Kniff finished his beer. The trick with the pepper still nagged at him, it was annoying to admit . . . and all those days spent searching in vain. These stupid Negroes seemed to know the lie of the land and how to move around. Who had taught them such tricks?

There was something not right, he'd thought it immediately.

Jim Kniff was uneasy.

He went back to the sheriff's office, told Old Johnson that if he liked, he could go home and rest his back while he kept watch over those two. Then he sat down heavily on the sheriff's chair, rested his feet on the desk, and pulled down his hat over his eyes to get some shut-eye. Half an hour would do fine, to digest the steak and beer.

Old Johnson had wished him goodnight, pausing for a moment at the door to look out at the street, breathe the fresh air and massage his aching back. If something happened, they'd come and find him at home, as they'd done before. Nothing unusual.

Jim Kniff had wanted to put his chickens in a cage, so let him keep an eye on them.

Despite the late hour, there was still a lot of noise coming from the saloons and taverns. The city was growing so fast: too many people, too many strangers, too much money, too many temptations. Old Johnson shook his head and went home. His sheriff's star needed to go to a younger man.

'Now,' said Peg Leg Joe. 'This is our chance. He's alone.'

'How are we going to free them?' asked Papa as the pair emerged from the pool of shadow of an old warehouse where they'd been hiding for the last two hours. The street was momentarily deserted. The only light came from the sheriff's office.

'There's only one way,' replied Peg Leg Joe, gripping the pistol. 'Go in by the main door, shove this under his nose, and make him give us the keys to the cell.'

'He'll never do it.'

'He will if he's convinced we'll use it. Got any other ideas?'

Sudden laughter and drunken voices reached them from the other end of the street. Then they heard a trotting horse approach, and had to wait until it went by.

'Now!'

'Give me that pistol,' said Papa. 'I'll do it.'

'What?'

'Jim Kniff mustn't see you. Mustn't know of your existence. Or else in a few days your ugly face will be stuck up in all the sheriffs' offices and every saloon within a radius of a hundred miles. You're big and fat Joe and have a wooden leg. Easy to recognise. They mustn't even suspect the existence of the Guides.'

'You've never used a pistol.'

'And I've never even threatened anyone. But I'll do it. I'm determined!'

Peg Leg Joe eyed Papa. An owl hooted from the warehouse roof.

'Man . . . OK take it. I'll go round the back. The four of us should come out from there.'

They emerged into the open.

'What time is it?' asked Mamma for the umpteenth time. There was no way of knowing.

The city had been dark and silent for hours, the moon was veiled. They had waited and waited . . . heart in mouth.

Going down Main Street following Mamma like chicks following a mother hen, they had walked as quickly as possible yet resisted the temptation to break into a run so as not to be noticed. They had dodged carts, cowboys smellier than their herds, half-drunk Negroes who had taken advantage of the liberties offered by the festival atmosphere and couldn't resist the temptation to pester a lone woman with three children in tow.

'Hey beauty, where you going?'

'Go away!' thought Tommy. 'Leave us alone . . . you of all people!'

Now it was Negro good for nothings creating problems.

Each time Mamma tugged at him and went on. Nothing could distract her, nothing could intimidate her. Peg Leg Joe had told her to go straight to the river without losing a minute. So she had gone right down Main Street, exited the city, and headed for the river as if she had never done anything else in her life.

She spotted an old hut falling to bits, its roof beams collapsed and wooden walls swollen with damp. They entered through a door hanging off its one hinge, closing it swiftly so nobody could see there was anyone in there. She spread an old blanket on the soft earth floor and hunkered down surrounded by the children. The accumulated fear, tension and anxiety of the last hours began to leak out of her and she trembled. They'd done it! Tommy thought his Mamma was pretty smart.

The river was nearby, hidden by the darkness and mist rising above it, but they were aware of its presence because of a damp watery smell. Every now and then waves slapped against the bank. The mist was invading the hut little by little and it was growing darker.

They made out a bridge with difficulty, the one they'd have to cross that same night, as soon as Papa and Peg Leg Joe and Sammy and Sarah appeared, if everything had gone well. But where were they?

Two lanterns gave off a feeble light at the entrance to the bridge: the bridge to freedom. The soldier on guard walked back and forth. Where were Papa and Peg Leg Joe? Had they been caught?

Mamma and the children were cold and hungry. The river damp had soaked their clothes. A boat's siren pierced the night, making them jump.

Tommy would have liked to comfort Mamma, giving her courage, and say, 'You'll see, everything will be alright.'

But he was made dumb by anguish. What would become of them if Papa and Peg Leg Joe didn't come? It would be up to him to take care of Mamma and his sisters, get them over the bridge, look for the next Station and find someone to help – leading them all the way to Canada.

Tommy wanted to become a Guide, didn't he? But right then he was just a scared little boy incapable of doing anything. 'What time is it?'

A creak. A squeak.

'Someone's there,' whispered Mamma. 'Don't move!'

There was shuffling at the door hanging off its hinges.

Another shuffling.

Whoever it was . . . was trying not to be heard, wanting to catch them unawares. The door squeaked. Two shadows, then three, outlined in the doorway, darker than the uncertain darkness of the night.

Then a wooden peg leg banging on the floor.

Peg Leg Joe. Papa. Sammy. Sarah . . . Hugs all round.

Questions came thick and fast.

'What happened?'

'Shhh! Someone might hear us.'

'Papa shot at Jim Kniff,' said Sammy with a smile that lit up the darkness. 'You should have seen him!'

Nineteen

Years later, Papa was bursting with pride as he recounted that episode to friends sitting round the kitchen table after a hearty supper prepared by Mamma. He puffed out his chest like a turkey cock and became at least five inches taller.

'I fired at him, yes sir. He was a bully that Jim Kniff. A big, fat thug. He frightened everybody. When Kniff went by everyone shut up. Right or not, son?'

'Yes, Papa.'

'What was I saying? It went like this. He'd caught Sammy and his wife Sarah, y'know Sarah don't you? Her over there, she's the one. He'd caught and locked 'em up in prison down there in that city – what's it called again? It'll come to me. Anyway, no hope for them. It'd all to end badly, that's for sure. You know as well as I do what happened to runaway slaves. So I say to Joe, the man with the wooden leg, we can't let this happen, man. I'm going to set them free. If you're afraid, you don't have to come, I'll manage on my own. That's what I said. True or not, son?'

'Yes, Papa,' replied Tommy.

'So I took my old six shooter –I always had it with me 'cause you never know what might happen – I hugged Mamma and the children and told Tommy to look after his sisters. I said to them, "I've never left anyone behind." That's what I said. And I gave that bully Jim Kniff a lesson. True or not, son?'

'Yes, Papa,' said Tommy trying hard not to burst out laughing.

Papa had waited until Peg Leg Joe stationed himself behind the back door and then went into the sheriff's office, his heart thumping and the pistol weighing as heavy as a stone in his hand.

Jim Kniff was snoring in the sheriff's swivel chair as he digested his dinner. Alongside him was a stove with a pot of coffee, gone cold. Above him was a gun rack secured with a heavy padlock. And on the wall were the Wanted posters, featuring a row of ugly faces with the inscription:

WANTED

and the value of the reward in big letters:

$100, $250 . . .

Papa had seen Sarah and Sammy in the cell at the back. As he came in, they leapt up from the bench where they were sitting looking miserable, and rushed to clutch at the cell bars.

Papa had seen everything and nothing on account of the sweat pouring into his eyes. He was concentrating on holding the gun upright, and thinking about what he should say. His tongue was stuck to the roof of his mouth. He was speechless.

The door banged shut. Jim Kniff, woken from his nap, had grunted and pushed back his hat off his eyes, scratched his head, and looked at the intruder who had disturbed him. His mouth dropped open in shock: a Negro!

The Negro pointed a gun at him, 'Please, Master Jim, open up the cell . . .'

Papa had called every white man he had ever encountered 'Master', because that's what a slave did. 'Yes Master, no Master . . .'

So he did it now, too, while pointing a gun at the white man.

Jim Kniff could not believe his eyes, a Negro was threatening him! He started to laugh at the sight of a stupid, dirty Negro armed with a gun. Where did he get hold of it?

He didn't even know how to hold it. He was trembling like he had a fever. Negroes couldn't use a gun. What an idea! Cowards and good for nothings, the lot of them. Then he got tremendously angry. He'd teach that animal a lesson. He'd make him pay dearly, and give him a lesson he'd never forget.

A Negro threatening a white man – him, Jim Kniff!

'Please, Master Jim, open up that cell,' repeated Papa.

Jim Kniff advanced on Papa with great strides, he was raging now. Ready to throttle him with his bare hands.

Papa closed his eyes and fired somewhere in the direction of Jim Kniff's boots to scare him. He would never have fired at a man, not even Jim Kniff, to save his own life. A sour smell of smoke and powder from the shot filled the sheriff's office.

Papa opened his eyes.

The bullet had grazed Jim Kniff's right boot, rebounded off the floor and hit his spur, which was still rotating.

Jim Kniff was paralysed with amazement. His thoughts went round in a circle.

'A Negro has shot at me!'

'A Negro has shot at me!'

'**A Negro has shot me!**'

The spur's wheel whirled giddily around.

Tiiiiinggggggg!

       Tiiiiinggggggg!

Then he felt a breath of air brush his ears as if someone had opened the back door, and heard a strange, unidentifiable noise.

Tap . . .

  Tap . . .

    Tap . . .

It was as if a stick or a wooden leg was hitting the floor. But how could that be?

BAM!

He couldn't hear anything else because his big body crashed to the floor, like a tree felled by a storm, and he didn't move again.

Peg Leg Joe lowered the banjo which he'd used as a club, looked at Jim Kniff, then looked at Papa.

'Let's hope it's not damaged,' he said worriedly, stroking his instrument. 'You know, it's very delicate. It only needs a small thing to ruin it.'

'Let's hope not,' said Papa.

They looked at Jim Kniff on the floor.

'Perhaps we should tie him up,' the Guide proposed, taking the lasso hanging on the back of the chair.

'You know, when he wakes up he's going to have a very bad headache. And he'll be very angry.'

'You think so?'

'You bet!'

'Get us out of here!' interrupted Sammy through the cell bars.

'Hold it, said 'Peg Leg Joe". 'What's the hurry?'

Papa was strutting about, gun in hand, 'Yes, what's the hurry?'

The bridge was long, the opposite end lost somewhere in the night mist, impossible to see. Down below, the river water ran swift and muddy, making a loud noise.

The two navigation lights gave out a ghostly yellow glow.

'Now what?' asked Papa.

'The guard walks back and forth, see? Each time, he takes twenty steps before turning, not one less. I've counted them. We have the time of twenty steps to cross the bridge to the other side. We'll leave in groups.'

'The bridge is longer than twenty steps. We won't make it.'

'It's too dark for him to see us. The mist will protect us. The noise of the river will cover our footsteps. And we have no choice. Remember: freedom is on the other side.'

'Let's go,' said Papa. 'Mamma is with me. Tommy, look after your sisters.'

Every eye was fixed on the guard, spying on his every movement. He seemed very young, a lanky lad with long fair hair, he walked like a goose, chest stuck out, with his rifle over his shoulder.

Twenty paces one way.

About-turn . . .

Twenty paces back.

About-turn . . .

He had on a military jacket with a farmhand's trousers and a cowhand's boots.

'They don't use soldiers on this duty,' explained Peg Leg Joe. 'They're kids from the State Militia. He's colder than us and just as frightened. But beware: he won't hesitate to use that shotgun, even though he's afraid.'

'Are we going?'

'We're going. Wait . . .' said Peg Leg Joe.

'Go – now!'

Mamma and Papa climbed heavily up the three steps leading to the entrance to the bridge. The soldier had already taken four steps . . . five . . . six.

Mamma was slow, too slow . . . so exhausted after all those weeks of travelling. It was as though all the emotions, fear and tension of the last day had finally drained her of energy, leaving her empty. Papa had to support her.

They set off along the bridge. Slow, too slow.

Eight . . . nine . . . ten.

Tommy counted the steps one at a time.

They weren't far enough across.

Then the moon suddenly emerged from behind the clouds that had been hiding it. The mist momentarily evaporated. It was as though a bright light had illuminated the two fugitives. The guard would see them!

Twelve . . . thirteen . . . fourteen. Or was it fifteen?

'They're not going to make it,' said Peg Leg Joe.

He picked up a pebble, threw it in a wide arc so that it fell in front of the soldier, and then rolled down the bank to splash into the water.

The beanpole stopped in his tracks, and looked right and left.

He took a few steps and said in a hesitant voice, 'Who goes there?'

He waited in vain for a reply, moved cautiously towards the river bank, and peered into the darkness.

'Who goes there?' he asked again in a shrill voice, nervously clutching at his gun. He scratched his head, stood uncertain for a moment, then turned and resumed his pacing.

Mamma and Papa had already gone down off the other end of the bridge. The moon went back into hiding, the mist thickened its tentacles.

They all crossed over, one little group at a time, without the goose with his gun over his shoulder noticing.

They were on the other side!

'We're in Illinois,' said Peg Leg Joe. 'It's not Canada yet, but the slaves here are free!'

'Hallelujah!' everyone chorused.

'Captain Archer and Jim Kniff can't touch us here, but the journey is still a long one, and there are many people here as well who'd willingly harm us. But with God's help, we're almost in Canaan.'

Everyone stayed silent for several minutes, thinking of their long journey, finally over. Of the plantation and the cabins. Of the ones left behind. Of an unimaginable, uncertain future. Of different dangers and difficulties. Of those who had made the journey before them, but had failed.

They thought about many things.

Then Papa went to Peg Leg Joe and hugged him.

'Joe,' he began, 'Joe . . . I wanted . . . we wanted . . .'

'Aaaahhhhh! Don't come all soppy on me. On we go. There's still a good way to go. And you, little man, have skipped a lesson. Tomorrow a double session.'

'But I . . .'

'Silence!'

The first Station in Illinois which welcomed them a few miles further on, was a Baptist church which, strangely, was left open in the dead of night. They found food, blankets, clothes and everything needed for the last part of the journey.

After they had eaten, they asked Peg Leg Joe to sing to them. After he'd tuned the banjo which seemed not to have suffered from its encounter with Jim Kniff's hard head, he sang – at last! – a happy song which was in keeping with the mood of that day, and with which everyone joined in, clapping their hands and stamping their feet in time:

Oh when the Saints
Go marching in
Oh when the Saints
Go marching in
Lord I want to be in that number
When the Saints
Go marching in . . .

Tommy imagined that those Saints on the march were all the slaves in Alabama, Tennessee and Ohio and the other places he didn't know about: all those who at sunrise of the new day would be bent over in the cotton fields; would be trembling in fear in the darkness of damp kitchens; all the children, especially in places he didn't know about, who like him wanted to be free, and to learn how to read and write so they could understand people and things and the world.

He got so enthusiastic he made Peg Leg Joe give him the banjo and tried to repeat the chords of the song. Then he cleared his throat noisily and attacked the final verse. He had hardly got halfway through than he saw Peg Leg Joe stuffing his fingers in his ears and pretending to look desperate.

'What did I tell you?' he said, turning to the others who nodded,

'A cow. He's as out of tune as a cow just before milking.'

Twenty
Alabama, May 1857

The young man walking along the dusty lane leading through the fields to the village was very funny-looking: very very tall, very very thin, covered in dust and carrying a gourd slung across his back.

The first person to intercept him was Bessie who was nine years old and had plaits tied with coloured ribbons. She was sitting on the edge of an oak wood, keeping an eye out for the fox that roamed around the cabins every night in search of food. She didn't want to harm the fox, she just wanted to have a little chat with it. She had also slipped out of the house one night – strictly not allowed – to give it a present of a little mouthful she'd set aside for precisely that reason.

But the fox didn't trust her. Even now the fox was hiding and was only waiting for Bessie to go away – or to be distracted – to clear off.

Foxes – as you know – are cunning, but Bessie was very smart too. So she only glanced at the funny young man and immediately went back to concentrating on the den. The thing was, she wasn't really absolutely sure that the fox was inside. Maybe it had gone off for a walk, and she was waiting for nothing.

Meanwhile, the funny-looking young man had reached her and stopped beside her.

He took a big handkerchief from his pocket and wiped away the sweat. 'What are you doing?'

'Ssssshhhhh!' said Bessie without turning round.

That's all she needed! He'd scare the fox away. Assuming it was in there.

'There's no fox,' said the young man sitting next to her. 'Right now foxes are out hunting.'

'How do you know?'

'I've known lots of foxes.'

Bessie looked at the young man, then again at the den. In truth, she was fed up of staying still, just waiting.

'Sure?' she asked.

'Almost.'

Bessie had to admit that 'almost' was an honest answer.

'Have you come from over there?' she asked, pointing.

'Yes.'

'Did you pass by the crossroads? Mamma Brigitte's there!'

The funny-looking young man shrugged.

'I've got my lucky charm. Do you want to see it? It's a lightning point. Look. Not even Mamma Brigitte can do anything against it. It keeps you safe from the Evil Eye and . . .'

'You're not tricking me,' said Bessie. 'That's not a lightning point. There aren't any. It's an arrowhead.'

'That's not true!' protested the young man.

'Yes it is!'

Almost all adults were silly, to tell the truth, and they were always trying to trick you. But they couldn't do it to her.

'Who's in charge?' asked the young man.

'That's a really silly question,' answered Bessie.

'Everyone knows it's Master Bennett in charge here.'

The young man gave a big grin.

'You're right,' he said. 'It really is a silly question.'

'Uh huh,' went Bessie.

She went back to looking at the den. What if the fox was still in there?

'Do you know what this is?' asked the young man, showing her the gourd.

Bessie looked sidelong at it, then at the den, then peeped at the gourd again.

In the end, curiosity got the upper hand. Bessie was very curious.

'It's a musical instrument,' the young man explained. 'It's called a banjo.'

'Uh huh,' went Bessie.

'Would you like me to teach you a song?'

'Depends,' said Bessie. 'What's it about?'

'Saints who go marching to freedom.'

'I don't know what freedom is,' said Bessie cautiously. But she liked songs.

'I didn't know either,' said the young man. 'But then I learned. A man with a wooden leg taught me it. If you want, I'll tell you.'

A man with a wooden leg really was something interesting.

'Uh huh,' said Bessie. She liked stories too, and the funny-looking young man seemed like he knew a heap of them.

Who knew what it was all about, this story of freedom. What if he were to tell it that evening? She took Tommy by the hand and started off home.

Featured Songs

All the songs referred to in the story are available
to listen to online:

Follow the Drinking Gourd
Written by Peg Leg Joe and sung by Richie Havens

Steal Away
Sung by Mahalia Jackson and Nat King Cole
or by Michelle Williams

Oh, Freedom
Sung by Harry Belafonte

When the Saints Go Marching In
Sung by Louis Armstrong
or by Elvis Presley
or by Bruce Springsteen